The Croaking of the Raven

FRANCIS LYALL

The Croaking of the Raven

St. Martin's Press
New York

For Heather

Library of Congress Cataloging-in-Publication Data

Lyall, Francis.
　　The croaking of the raven / Francis Lyall.
　　　　p.　　cm.
　　ISBN 0-312-06940-5
　　I. Title.
　PR6062.Y29C76　1992
　823′.914—dc20
　　　　　　　　　　　　　　　　　　　　　　　　　　91-34087
　　　　　　　　　　　　　　　　　　　　　　　　　　CIP

First published in Great Britain by William Collins Sons & Company Limited.

First U.S. Edition: January 1992
10 9 8 7 6 5 4 3 2 1

CHAPTER 1

FRIDAY

'He's not very good.'

Drew was surprised at Felicity's soft comment as they watched the amateur magician attempt to palm a five of hearts. Usually she was tolerant of imperfection, and in any case he thought the magician was doing rather well.

'They like him all right,' he whispered, nodding his head towards the children sitting on the floor in front of the bandstand. Among them Morag, their elder, was fidgeting, but Gwen was enthralled even though she had seen the act before at the 'farewell' party the previous Friday evening. Saturday was change-over day, and the party was the traditional end-of-the-week event at the Monzie Hydro. Later there would be the prizes for the bowls, tennis and golf competitions and after that there would be a dance, but the early part of the evening belonged to the children.

Felicity wrinkled her brow.

Drew leaned back in his chair. The Hydro was an excellent large family hotel, just the place for a couple with young children. It had a feeling of solidity, of age even although it was not more than a hundred years old. It provided entertainment and solitude, games and walks, supervision if wanted and in its extensive grounds the kids could run safe and free without disturbing other guests.

Drew smiled to himself. Part of his holiday reading had been a history of the place he had found in the Library and he wondered how the Victorian builder of the Hydro would have viewed the antics of the present guests: but then he had obviously had a hard practical streak, which could have been summed up in 'give the customer what he wants', so perhaps he would have approved.

The young man persisted with the children. Unfortunately there was one precocious youngster in the front row who took rhetorical questions as genuine, and another who was shrilly convinced that 'It's up your sleeve!' Even so, the majority of the children seemed entranced.

It had been a good two weeks. They had walked. He had golfed. They had made various trips—to the glass-factory, to the hydro dam up in a glen where the swifts, nesting under the eaves of the sluice-control building, had swooped fearlessly round them. They had 'done' a couple of National Trust properties and been to a wild life park. Morag and Gwen had ridden. He had putted, played tennis and swum with the kids. Morag was getting to be quite a young seal. The pressures of work had eased. Indeed, over the week he had come into such a benign frame of mind that he had raised no obejction when that morning on his return from the golf course Felicity had announced that they were going down to Monzie to see about getting him a new sports jacket. He ran his hand down a sleeve and gently rearranged the lapel, ignoring the smile that twitched at the corner of his wife's mouth. Briefly he wondered what his colleagues would say when he walked in with a new jacket, for to say he was sartorially conservative was an understatement and this one was, by his standards, loud. Further, he tended to live in one jacket until Felicity quietly assassinated it. That thought made him smile. How appropriate for the wife of a forensic pathologist occasionally to engage in assassination. Or was it the slave trade? Two or three times he encountered a familiar jacket at a jumble sale. Once he had quietly bought it and restored it to his wardrobe. Nothing had been said.

His mind wandered again. It had been good to get away, and amusing to have bumped into Ian Crawford down in Monzie main street the other day—was it the Tuesday or the Wednesday? The Monzie chemist, the only purveyor of pills and potions to the hypochondriacs of Monzie and its hinterland of hotels and farms, had been burgled.

'Want to look?' Crawford had asked.

Drew had turned down the invitation. 'No,' he had replied. 'I need a break, and I'm having it. Don't remind me of the real world.' But even so, professional curiosity had prompted him. 'Much taken?'

Crawford had shrugged. 'Selective, as usual. Amphetamines—anti-depressants—some hypodermics. We're getting a list.'

Drew had briefly considered relenting. If Crawford was here, so probably was Alan Mason, though a chemist burglary was not his usual field.

Crawford was quick on the uptake. 'I'm down with Chief Inspector Shepherd,' he said. 'Superintendent Mason's involved in the Royal visit. I've been borrowed for the day.'

'Ah,' said Drew. He remembered seeing that some minor royalty was opening a new office block in Greyhavens. 'Well, I hope Alec Shepherd returns you in good working order. Still, I'd better be on my way. Felicity'll be waiting for me.'

'Have a good holiday, then.'

'I will. Especially knowing you lot are working,' Drew said, smiling.

He wondered whether his colleagues had made any progress. There had been a number of burglaries at chemists in the region recently. Alec Shepherd was usually not involved. He dealt with drug-trafficking. But then, Drew remembered vaguely, it had been decided to take all drug-related crimes under one umbrella. That must explain it.

*

The conjuror was finished, and they were moving on to the presentation of the prizes for the various competitions which had run over the week.

Felicity frowned slightly at the presentation of a box of chocolates to the winners of the Men's Doubles.

'You should have had that,' she whispered.

'They were very good,' he replied.

'No,' she whispered back. 'Last week, I mean. I don't know what happened to Roy. He's a better tennis player than a conjuror.'

Drew shrugged. It was true that something had happened. He hadn't wanted to play, but Morag and Gwen had insisted he enter the competition. To his brief relief there had been a chance of escape when there hadn't been a partner for him, but Roy had said he would play with him. Then, in the second round, something had happened.

'I still think he threw the match,' Felicity went on. 'You and he were doing too well. It wouldn't do for the hotel's games organizer to win the tennis.'

Drew shook his head. He thought Roy had been trying hard to make his shots. He had great sympathy with his partner. When your tennis starts to go, trying to correct it mid-match often makes things abruptly worse. Oh, he had seen Roy turn moody with other people, losing interest or impatient with indifferent partners, but Drew's own tennis was quite good. No, whatever had affected Roy, the opposition had been just too good.

They applauded all the winners, one in particular getting sustained clapping from Drew's girls. This, the winner of the women's singles, was an attractive mid-twenties with long black hair whose languorous looks belied a startling ability to get about a tennis court. She had made friends with the girls, giving them some gratuitous coaching from which Morag at least had profited.

Eventually the presentations were over and the band

started up. The Conga was a tradition of the Monzie Hydro, and marked the end of the 'children's' section of the Friday evening party. Gwen rushed up to him, and he unwillingly joined the long procession that snaked its way out of the ballroom, round the corridors, through the dining-room, round the snack bar, out on to the enclosed balcony, back in through the lounge and so back to the ballroom where everybody applauded everyone else.

'Right,' came Roy's voice from the amplifier. 'Thanks to everyone for a gorgeous week. We're sorry some of you are leaving tomorrow, but we hope to see you all next year. Now we'll have *Aul' Lang Syne*, and then a break to allow the kiddies to get off to bed.'

After *Aul' Lang Syne* Roy went over to the door, saying farewell to the various families he knew were to depart the following morning.

'See you next year?' he asked Morag as she shyly approached.

'Don't know. It depends on Mummy and Daddy.'

'But you have had a good time?'

'Oh yes.'

'Yes. We have,' said Drew. 'I'm glad we came.'

'Your first time here?'

Drew nodded.

'You'll be back, then.' The voice was confident. 'They say we don't often have single visit families.'

'Oh. Do I gather this is your first year?' asked Felicity.

'Yes. With luck I'll be back next year. But they don't need a year-round organizer.'

'So what do you do during the winter?' Drew asked.

'I'm not sure what I'll do this year. Probably go back to Spain or down into North Africa—Egypt maybe. I've always had a hankering to see Egypt.'

'This job must pay well if you can afford that.'

Roy laughed.

The black-haired girl came over and smiled at Roy as she joined the group.

'I'm off too,' she said.

'Can we give you a lift into Greyhavens?' asked Felicity.

'Please come, Lucy,' chipped in Gwen eagerly.

'That's very good of you,' said the girl, 'but I'm being looked after.' She glanced at Roy, who nodded.

A faint smile flickered over Felicity's lips. She had seen them together in a yellow sports car and thought there was something between these two. She was glad to have her suspicions confirmed.

'Oh well,' she said. 'In any event I suppose you'll be quicker to go over to Birley. But I wanted to thank you again, Lucy, for what you've done for Morag's service.'

'It's a pleasure to be able to partner her at doubles and not to feel under threat when she's serving,' laughed Drew.

'And I want you to be sure and come and see us if you ever come to Greyhavens,' Felicity continued. 'Have you got a card?' she asked Drew.

He groped in his wallet, produced a card and held it out.

'Business, I'm afraid,' he said, 'but our home address is in the left-hand corner. Oh yes. Just a minute.' He took the card and altered the phone number before handing it over. 'They've put in a new exchange and we've got a new number. But like any good Greyhavnor, I'm still using up my stock.'

The girl took the card and read it. She looked up at him sharply but said nothing.

Drew noticed, but also said nothing. He was used to odd reactions when people got to know his occupation. Only a few made no comment whatever, but he had found that invariably these were the people he liked best. He was glad she had met that test.

'Well,' he said, getting his daughters by the neck. 'These two are for bed, and then Felicity and I are going to have a last walk up the Knoll. It's marvellous to be able to walk straight out on to a hill like that.'

'And the views are wonderful,' said Lucy.

'Especially the sunsets.'

Courtesies were exchanged and the Drew family went off upstairs.

The sun had set, but the sunset was not yet finished as the Drews set off past the fountain, between the tennis courts and on and up through the self-catering accommodation.

'Another year I would quite be prepared to come to one of these,' said Felicity as they passed the A-frames.

'Perhaps.'

Above the upper road they struck off up the steep footpath rather than go round to the easier route. Drew was pleased with himself. He was barely feeling the strain. When they had arrived two weeks before, their first time up the hill had worried him. He had found himself puffing and sweating. Now he was fit again.

At the indicator on the top they looked round the panorama. All was quiet, save for the odd whistling flight of a bird making for its roost. To the north and west the mountains loomed.

'There he goes,' said Felicity suddenly, pointing down the north slope.

Through a gap in the trees Drew saw the white vest of the runner as he pounded his way along the track which wound its way round the Knoll from the end of the upper road.

'That's every night we've seen him,' she remarked.

'Well, at least he's fit,' he said.

'Of course he's fit. He's a fitness fanatic.'

'Unlike me.'

Felicity raised her arms shoulder high and, spreading them slightly outward, pivoted slowly.

'Yes. This has been a good place. I'm glad Alan Mason told us about it.'

'I'll tell him on Monday.'

'Will you see him?'

'Bound to. I don't expect crime has gone on holiday just because we have.'

She laughed.

They went over to the south face, where the Knoll dropped sheer for a hundred feet or so into the forest that ran the quarter-mile or so to the edge of the town of Monzie. The town itself, picked out by its street lights, was as if laid out for their inspection. Away out in the valley they saw the lights of other villages.

'Why can't we see Greyhavens?' asked Felicity.

Drew gestured to the east. 'It's over that way, but it's too far to see.' He pointed to one set of lights about half way to the horizon. 'If that's PenIron, which I think it is, then the glow away behind it to the right might be Birley. Greyhavens would be tucked away round the end of the hills. Too far to see its glow except maybe in winter when the sky's darker. About thirty miles as the crow flies. More by that awful road.'

Felicity, looking down, shivered. The tops of the trees below them were becoming indistinct in the gathering shadows.

'I don't like it here when it's like that. There's almost an attraction. You can quite understand how people fall over places like that.'

He was grateful for the excuse. As he had got older, he had found that his appetite for heights had shrunk, but he never admitted that even to his wife—though somehow he thought she had guessed.

Sedately and comfortably together, they went back to the hotel. As they did so, back at Greyhavens Colin Brown set out about what he called his 'business'.

CHAPTER 2

SATURDAY

1

Although it was their last day Drew came down as usual early and alone to breakfast. He had found that if he got into the dining-room at 8.15 he could be on the first tee at the hotel's small nine-hole golf course at the other side of the Knoll by about ten to nine, and finished by quarter past ten. When he had wakened it was to find a beautiful day, and one final round would just finish things off nicely. They did not have to check out until eleven, and the packing was virtually finished.

One of the beauties of being first on the course was that there were always the rabbits to be seen on the eighth and ninth fairways. These ran along the side of the hill and were bounded by ancient broken stone dykes with thick gorse and bracken up behind them. He had lost several golf balls into that jungle, but it clearly was paradise for the rabbits. One morning he had counted over sixty grazing quietly as he made his way along the second and back along the fifth. But always as he emerged on to the spine of the course along the sixth, they would scatter and flee, only the hardiest (or most foolhardy) remaining until he drove off on the seventh. Then there were those curious four or five light brown ones. Were they escapes from captivity which had managed to find their way to those warrens? Or were they sports among the local population? Or maybe some child had decided to set free some pets. There could be many explanations.

He was buttering his morning roll when his reverie was interrupted.

'Dr Drew. It is "Doctor" isn't it?'

Drew looked up. The tall, spare figure of Paton, the manager of the hotel, was standing beside his table.

'Are you a medical doctor?'

'Yes.'

'I wonder, then. Could you come and help us? Until our own usual man gets up from the village.'

'Surely,' replied Drew, getting to his feet. 'What's the matter?'

'This way, please.'

Quickly Drew was conducted out of the dining-room, up the stairs which immediately faced its door, and then up the smaller flight which led to the passage which he knew ran above the dining-room. The door at the end of the passage was open. His professional instincts stirring, Drew noted that the room number was 126.

Inside a maid was sitting on the bed, her face in her hands. An older woman—a supervisor perhaps—had her arm around the girl. A tray with tea and rolls stood beside a portable typewriter, both placed awkwardly on the dressing-table.

On the other side of the bed the corner door into the bathroom was open and the light was on, the Xpelair droning quietly.

'In there,' said Paton.

Drew went round the bed and over to the open door.

There was a body in the bath. The water was deep. A book, a teapot and a cup and saucer were in the water. It looked as if they had fallen from the soap rack which was in front of the body, one end still at the edge of the bath. The teabag had floated loose and was beside one ankle. The body itself was slumped down into the water. Probably the knees had upset the soap rack. The head was tilted forward and to the left.

Automatically Drew put his hand into the water. It was cold. He moved the head back. A bruised welt on the left jaw and cheek extended to the upper left lip. Drew sucked his breath through his lips and teeth, making a 'tsk' sound.

Paton was in the doorway, watching.

He came in. 'Shall I pull the plug?' he asked.

'No. Not yet.'

Drew squatted beside the bath, his frame concealing the head from the watcher. He recognized the man as someone —presumably a guest—he had seen around the hotel. He did not know his name, but his impression was of a choleric sort of individual. He thought he remembered hearing him bawl out some member of the staff or other.

He eased the head back to its original position and got up.

'Look,' he said to Paton, who was staring at the top of the head. 'I'm not entirely happy about this. I want you to phone the local police and get them to send someone up. Say Dr Drew of the Greyhavens Force asked you to do that —they'll recognize the name. Lock the room, and put someone outside it until the local man gets here. In the meantime I'll do some phoning myself.'

The manager dragged his attention back to him. 'You mean . . .?' He looked worried.

'Possibly. I can't be sure without some tests. It's unlikely. It could be natural causes, but we go through the routine in any sudden death like this.'

'I didn't realize you were with the police. So that's why the name was familiar. I am sorry to have brought you back to work without you even getting home from your holiday.'

Drew shrugged, part of him whole-heartedly agreeing. No matter. He had been involved, and his professional instincts were telling him that this one needed further

probing. In the meantime he would have to tell Felicity that
she would have to drive the family home.

2

'Good,' said Superintendent Mason as he surveyed the
room. 'Nothing's been moved. That's how I like to see
things.'

'I'm not sure nothing has been touched. The maid was
in first and then the supervisor,' replied Drew. 'But we'll be
able to find out what they touched, if anything.'

'All right. Well, perhaps if you take the body away you
can see if your instinct was right or not.' Mason smiled,
his broken left eyebrow arching devilishly. He would be
surprised if Drew found his suspicion to be baseless: he had
never known him to be wrong . . . as yet.

'Fine,' said Drew. 'The manager asked us to take it down
the luggage lift and out through the lower doors. I saw the
ambulance come in just a minute or so ago, I think. I'll go
down and check.'

'Yes. That would be best. There is no need to alarm the
guests, and I'm sure Paton would prefer we are as low-profile
as possible.'

'All right. I'll be back anon.'

'Now, Ian,' said Mason to his assistant as Drew left.
'Once the body's away, let's have an inventory of this room.
I want everything down on the list, and a note of content
in the case of books and suchlike. When you've got something like this, anything that can help us to get to know
what kind of person we had here can be useful. If we know
all we can about the victim it might just point to the killer
—if killer there was. Who else have we got with us?'

'Paget and a couple of constables.'

'Umm. Well, we'll probably need more than that. Saturday's a bad day here. If memory serves, it's change-over

day. We'll need to find out everyone who has left, particularly anyone from this corridor.' He looked at his watch. 'There'll maybe be some still not checked out as well. Get them all spoken to. Get Paget on to that. And ask Greyhavens for some help either from there or from Birley. I'll have a look round here.' Mason went across to the window. The view was magnificent, as he had expected from such an end room.

Crawford nodded, pursing his lips slightly. If this was a case requiring further action there was going to be a lot of dogged slogging to be done. The hotel was large. On the way down to it Mason had commented that he reckoned that there might be as many as four hundred guests, and about fifty staff. That could be a nightmare if there was nothing clear to go on.

He went off to start Paget on listing all the people who had left that morning already. As he returned from that errand, Drew emerged from the luggage lift along with a couple of ambulance men and a stretcher.

3

Mason surveyed the room. It was oblong, the door in what he thought of as the bottom right-hand corner. Two windows in the long outside wall opposite were separated by the dressing-table. The bed was behind the door facing the dressing-table. The picture above the bed was a pastoral scene—a Constable perhaps, thought Mason without checking. The door into the bathroom was in the left-hand corner of the short wall on the other side of the bed. A television set was in the far corner, with an easy chair beside it. On the other short wall, immediately in front of the door, as it were, there was a chest of drawers, and beyond it a utility shelf on which there was a kettle, still plugged in, and the usual accoutrements for tea or coffee. Presumably that was where the deceased had brewed his last cup.

He looked at the dressing-table with the morning tea-tray perched uneasily beside the typewriter, a couple of books and some sheets of paper. He was tempted to push the tray more securely on to the table from where the maid had clearly put it in her haste to see what might be wrong in the bathroom, then he smiled and touched nothing. Once as a junior officer he had made that mistake and had been 'roasted' when, with great difficulty, it had been established that a smudged print belonged to him.

Mason sat and waited.

It did not take long. Soon the body was on its way, and the Prints officer was working about the room. As he finished with one area, Crawford moved in to complete his inventory as instructed. Mason asked Prints to deal with the table, and got Crawford to list the material on it. Only then did he himself inspect the books and the paper. The books were new. Both were novels. The pile of paper was pristine. Two sheets which had been face down to the right of the typewriter contained a slashing review of one of them. The waste-paper basket held several discarded sheets, clearly drafts of the review. If the stratification of the crumpled sheets was a true indication of order of composition, what had been a fierce review had become progressively more cutting. The eventual 'final' version began:

The late Ambrose Bierce is reported to have reviewed a book with the simple sentence: 'The covers of this book are too far apart.' I am tempted to adopt his simplicity, but the crassness of this offering demands more fully to be stated.

The rest of the review fulfilled that demand.

As he read, Drew came back and went into the bathroom.

'What's his name?' asked Mason of no one in particular.

'Walter Emery,' replied Drew, coming back out.

'And?'

'And he's from somewhere down in England, according to the Manager. He lived in Cancaster, according to his registration card.'

'He's got a nice turn of phrase. Abrasive. Goes with his name, I suppose.' Mason passed the review to Drew who read it, snorting at the first paragraph.

'I like Bierce,' said Mason dreamily. 'His ghost stories are excellent, especially the ones to do with the Civil War.'

'Don't know him at all.'

'You must! Every intelligent person must have heard of Ambrose Bierce.'

'In that case I don't qualify,' said Drew, smiling. 'Well, I've just about finished, so I'll get back to Greyhavens and see what the body can tell me—unless there's a queue of others waiting for me.'

'OK. Go back in my car, and send it back for me, say for four o'clock.'

They went down in the lift together. Drew went out to the car, and Mason went to Reception. Paget was there.

'I've asked one particular couple to stay and see you,' he said. 'They were in 124. That's the room next door to the body.' Paget smiled; an older man, he sometimes took liberties with his younger but superior officer. Mason acknowledged it with a nod. Paget resumed. 'There's been a hundred and ninety-three checked out—eighty-one rooms in all. Some left before breakfast. I let a family in 98 go because they were driving to the north of England, and they said they knew nothing when I indicated why inquiries were being made. They'd heard nothing and seen nothing—not even the comings and goings once the thing blew up until you yourself came. I've got their address, and they seem genuine enough. And there are another four families from the West Wing who've waited till I had a word with you.'

Paget handed Mason two lists. 'These are the one's who've left, and the ones waiting.'

Mason scanned the second list, and handed it back.

'Fair enough,' he said. 'Let them go too. You did get a statement from the family in 98?'

'Yes. Of course.' Paget's tone made it clear that he did not think Mason should have felt he had to ask that question.

Mason smiled. 'Just testing,' he said lightly. 'What about the staff. How many are there?'

Paget's mouth thinned. 'One hundred and seventy-one,' he replied. 'That's counting all the part-timers as well. There's fifty-eight living on the premises—full-timers mostly.'

Mason whistled, then shrugged. 'Nothing for it, I'm afraid. You'll need to go through them all. I'll get extra help down from Greyhavens. There just might be something one of them can tell us.' His tone briskened. 'Now, where have you got the family from . . . was it 124?'

'That's right.'

4

Mason was not well received.

'What's going on. Why can't we leave?' said a man getting to his feet as he entered the room. A woman sat with a toddler on her knee. The child solemnly inspected the intruder.

Mason raised a placating hand. 'No one's stopping you leaving, Mr Scott,' he said.

'Good. Come on, Maisie.' To Mason he said, 'You'll hear more about this—this interference with our liberty.' He was beginning to splutter. His wife was still sitting down and the child had turned to bury its face in her bosom. Mason addressed her.

'I am most sorry to have prevented your getting on

your way, but there is a serious matter in hand. I am
Superintendent Mason of the Greyhavens Police. I'm here
because there has been a fatality overnight in the room next
door and we're not quite sure about it.'

The man sat down, a puzzled expression struggling to
overcome his scowl.

'How can we help?' the woman asked quietly.

'Well,' said Mason slowly. 'How would it be if we were
to start last night. Did you hear anything during the night?
Or during the evening, come to that?'

The man snorted.

'What sort of things?' The woman's voice was quiet.

'Sounds. Argument in the corridor. Anything like that?'

'Well . . .' the voice was hesitant.

'She stopped me,' the man burst out. 'I'd have sorted
them out. But she stopped me.'

'Stopped you doing what?'

'There was some noise again from the room next door,'
intervened the woman. 'Donald wanted to go and complain,
but I said it was our last night. And it did quieten down
quite quickly.'

Mason took out a notebook. 'About what time would this
have been?'

'Here.' The man had got to his feet again. His eyes were
on the notebook. 'We're not getting mixed up in anything.'

'You're not mixed up in anything so far as I know. It's
just as I said. There has been a death and we have to look
into such things.' Mason turned to the woman. 'You said
that there was some noise "again". What did you mean by
"again"? Had it happened before?'

The man laughed shortly. 'I'll say. There was always
noise coming from that room this last week.'

'Now Donald, don't exaggerate,' the woman replied
quickly. Then she said to Mason: 'But it is true, what
Donald says. There were a couple of evenings this last week

when I heard what sounded like an argument going on. It's a matter of Sarah, you see. She doesn't go to sleep well when she's not at home. Does she, my pet?' She jogged the child up and down.

'And?'

'And I usually came upstairs immediately after dinner and sat with her until she was well asleep. We left her in the Nursery till I was done, and then we came up and had our bath, didn't we, pet?'

The 'pet' nodded solemnly. 'We'se stories,' she confided, and then hid her face in her mother.

Mason smiled.

'So just when I've been sitting here all quiet like, there would come voices from next door.'

'What sort of voices?'

'Sounded like a quarrel.'

'And last night, Mrs Scott? Was that later, if your husband heard it too?'

'Yes, Sherlock,' said the man. 'It was. It was about half ten or so when I came back. A couple of fellows and I had been down to the Burnside Inn having a game of darts. When I got back there was this argument going on. And I was going to sort them out.'

'It can be very upsetting,' said Mason.

'But it stopped,' said the woman. 'The door went and it stopped.'

'I see. I see.' Mason put his notebook away and went to the phone. 'There's just one more thing I need,' he said.

'Oh, that's right. I forgot,' said the woman. 'My mother phoned in the middle of it.'

Mason laughed at the expression on her face. 'No, I'm not psychic,' he said. 'I'm asking for someone to come up and we'll get you to estimate what the sound of the door was like.' He dialled through to Paget.

Shortly afterwards it was established that even making

an allowance for a quiet evening the door to Room 126 must have been slammed with considerable force to have caused the noise that had been heard in 124.

5

'I'm sorry to be here in such circumstances. It's always been so pleasant to cast work aside when I've been here in the past, but . . .' Mason shrugged and sat down in the chair beside Paton's desk.

'I'm sorry too, Superintendent,' said the Manager, pouring out coffee. 'None of us likes having a death or even a serious illness, though it comes to all of us in this line of business. I'm afraid we find having the police in a little upsetting. But we'll do what we can. Would you like lunch here? I'm sure we could fit you in.'

'That would be convenient. Presumably you do have gaps on change-over day.'

Paton smiled. 'Yes, indeed. And there is of course the gap left by Dr Emery. Milk? Sugar?'

'Both, please. Not much milk. Yes. I quite understand, your position. We'll do our best to minimize our presence, but things have to be gone into. I was wondering if you knew the deceased to any extent?' Mason continued as he ladled in the sugar.

Paton smiled. 'Dr Emery came here every year for the last eight years. I can give you exact dates.'

Mason showed surprise.

'It's not that difficult,' explained Paton. 'He came regularly, and I find that he always came for the last two weeks in June. Mind you, next year it would be more difficult. We've gone over to a computer this spring, and we won't have the ledgers any more.'

'So you'll have seen something of him over the years?'

'Something. Not much. He was always polite enough, but

never stopped really to have a chat, for all that he was always on his own. Rather uncommunicative.'

Mason caught the air of professional disappointment. 'Did you know anything about him at all, then?'

'Not really. I think he was in teaching or at a University or something. A University, I suppose. He once said something about liking to get away immediately the marking was over. I remember that when he came first he was very particular about being called "Dr Emery". He chewed out the front desk a couple of times, and complained to me. They had called him "Mr", and made out the forms in that way.' Paton laughed reflectively at the idiosyncrasies of mankind. 'But once that was past he was all right. His cheques didn't bounce.'

'Any complaints about noises from his room?'

'No. Why do you ask?'

'I've just been talking to the couple who were in 124. They said there was some disturbance a couple of times during the week and an argument and a slammed door last night.'

'Indeed. I'll ask around if you like.'

'Please. In the meantime we'll need to establish who the next of kin are and things like that.'

'That may be difficult.'

'How so?'

'I remember one time saying something about my wife or the children or something. I gathered from his reaction that there had been a messy divorce sometime in the past, and that he lost access to the child—a daughter, I think. That would be some explanation of his behaviour, perhaps.'

'Not really. But it might be that his behaviour was an explanation of the divorce. If he was that kind of man, a wife might want to get away.'

There was a pause.

Paton drummed his fingers on his desk. Mason waited,

recognizing the signs. He sipped his coffee and looked at the oil painting on the wall behind Paton. At length Paton spoke.

'It occurs to me that there is perhaps one person who just might be able to help you—or at least give you some more information about Dr Emery.'

Paton paused, but then, having committed himself, continued, speaking faster than his usual.

'It's one of our permanent folk. You've been here yourself. You know the ones I'm talking about. We've got at least one—well, there are more, but I would single out this one. Yes. We've got one unique character here as virtually a permanent resident. She has a room all the year over in the West Wing. Sometimes she goes off and "holidays" elsewhere . . .' Paton laughed, and Mason joined in politely. 'I would think she was away when you were here last summer—you were in August weren't you?'

Mason nodded, concealing his surprise. Had Paton been checking up on him as well?

'She's a Mrs Murgatroyd,' continued Paton. At least, that's her name now. She's been through a few husbands —at least four. And as a result she's very rich. All the husbands were in finance of one kind or another.'

'She must be getting on, then?'

'Oh, indeed. She must be in her late seventies.'

'And she got through four husbands? Before divorce was easy?'

'I think from what she's said over the years that they were all some years older than she was. Anyway she buried them all.'

The two men smiled.

'But that's not what's mainly interesting about her,' went on Paton. 'She was one of the Cliveden set. And in among Edward and Mrs Simpson. Some evenings, particularly during the winter, she'll invite me up to her room, and just sit and talk. I think she likes the company, not to say the audience, and . . .' Paton hesitated. 'I did Modern History myself at University and still read a lot of the books that are coming out—especially about the Abdication, and the social conditions just before the War. I think we were lucky not to have a revolution. Probably the War prevented that.'

'So how can she help?' interjected Mason. Paton was getting off the point. 'Are you saying that Emery was involved with Mrs Simpson? He couldn't be that old.' He smiled wryly.

'No. No. Indeed not. But she and Emery play—played —bridge as partners together when he came each year. Devastating they are—were. Or so I've been told. Perhaps she might know something about him that might help you.'

'Well, that might be interesting. Could you introduce me to her?'

'Yes, if you come back on Tuesday. I'm afraid that this weekend she has gone off to visit a friend in York and won't be back till late Monday and wouldn't be fit—or I dare say, willing—to see you until the next day.'

Mason got up.

'Well, thank you for what you've said. As it happens I've got a trial on Monday and won't be down here then. Perhaps if you could say to Mrs Murgatroyd that I will be coming I might see her some time during the Tuesday morning. I'll phone down and tell you exactly when I'm likely to get here.'

'Fine,' said Paton.

'I'm afraid there is one other thing. I'll need to have a complete list of staff.'

Paton nodded, pursing his lips.

'And anything you know about any of them,' went on Mason.

Paton sighed. 'That's difficult,' he said. 'Some have been here for years. Others come as casual labour—no references, nothing.'

'Well, I gather there's almost two hundred involved here
—any way to cut that down would be helpful.' Mason
crossed to the door.

'I'll see what I can do,' promised Paton.

6

Mason went back up to Room 126. Crawford was there
checking over his list.

'Good boy,' said Mason, grinning. 'I used to hate doing
that sort of job, but it has to be done. Never can tell when
something may emerge from a good little list.'

Crawford ran his hand through his hair and smiled wryly.
'Can you give me an example?'

'Oh yes,' said Mason expansively. 'I remember being told
by my instructor at Police College that he had once heard
from a friend that he had heard of someone who had known
someone whose wife's uncle had been on a case where a list
was important.'

'Indeed?'

'Yes. It was theft of some garments from a laundry, and
the laundry list was part of the evidence.'

Crawford grinned and closed his notebook with a snap.
'I'll get that typed up for you as soon as possible.'

'Fine. Anything occur to you about it yet?'

'No. It all seems standard to me. There's some pills and
so on that we'll need to check on, but everything else seems
standard. His dental fixative is foreign. That's all.'

'Foreign?'

'French.'

'Curious. Maybe he was over there recently and ran out.'

'Might be. But everything else in that line is virtually
new. He seems to be the sort that buys new to go on holiday.
But the fixative is well used.'

'I didn't know you knew French.'

'I don't.'

'Then how do you know that it's fixative?'

'It's got pictures on it.'

Mason sighed. 'I might have known it would be something simple. Well, if you've finished here, let's go down and have some lunch. The manager has got us a table in the dining-room—Dr Emery's, if you want to know.'

'Are you finished now?' The voice was hesitant. Mason looked round. A maid was at the door holding a small box.

'I don't want the room cleaned just yet,' said Mason.

'Oh no. I'm not here to do that. I'm just going round with the coffee, tea and milk,' said the girl, holding out the box. It was divided into sections with the various items on it. 'Would you mind if I do that now, in case I forget later?'

Mason glanced at the tray beside the kettle with its cup and biscuits. 'I suppose most folk take the tea and coffee with them,' he said. 'This needs both.'

'Almost everyone does when they leave, sir,' the maid said, putting down tea and coffee packets.

'But not the milk, I bet.'

'No. That tends to get left.' She spoke with an infectious smile.

'Especially if it's UHT,' replied Mason with a chuckle, which was matched by the others, and the three of them left the room in good humour.

7

Mason took his time over lunch. Crawford ate faster, listening while Mason outlined his conversation with the Scotts.

'You want to watch that,' Mason said, pointing with his fork at Crawford's empty plate. 'You'll end up with indigestion. Perhaps even with an ulcer. Take your time eating, and forget whatever is in the In-tray for a while. It's worth it. That, and a walk after lunch if you can manage it.' He pointed to the window. 'I'm going off for a few minutes after this. You can go later. I want you to phone Greyhavens while I'm gone and ask if there's anything come in while I've been here. Then you can get on with seeing such folk as may be available. Paget will have a list.'

'Anything you particularly want me to watch out for?'

'I don't think so. Looks routine to me. We want to know any occasions when Emery was seen in argument with anyone about the hotel, in the grounds or so on. Did anyone else hear any altercation on Friday night, to tie up with what the Scotts say they heard? Oh yes. I forgot as well to check what time the call in to the Scotts was logged at. That would give us a time for the argument, if there was one.'

'You think the Scotts got it wrong?'

'Not necessarily. But the wee man was fired up. He's the kind that if anything upsets his applecart, any distraction or annoyance will get out of proportion. I'm quite prepared to accept that there was a noise. Whether it amounted to the disturbance that they say it was is a different matter. Some other evidence would be useful.'

'Yes. All right. I'll do that.'

'Right. I'm going to stretch my legs,' he said to Crawford. 'It's too nice a day to miss out on the view. I'll be back in about half an hour.'

Crawford nodded. No such relief for him!

Mason went out by the main door and across the principal car park. He, Jane and their son Eric and had been on holiday at the Monzie Hydro a couple of years before, and he knew his way about.

He went along the small tarred road that led to the Manager's house and then along the track that it became once the house was passed. The track was dusty, but, although there had been no rain for some days, there were some patches of thick viscous mud caused by the drainage from the steep field on his right which sloped towards him.

There were horses grazing in the field, but they were far away near its top end. Here and there on the track he was on there were horse-droppings. Doubtless they marked the passing of horses from the hotel stable which used the path as one of their routes round the Knoll. The field on his left was more level and had sheep in it. On the other side of it trees masked the village from view.

The track rose as it bent round the end of the Knoll, and then split. Before it did so Mason was surprised, disappointed and enchanted. What he had remembered as a small stand of ancient Scots pines huddling themselves against the winds coming down the valley had been devastated. Just where the hill bent it was as though shears had been taken to the plantation. A few split and broken stumps showed it was wind and not the hand of man that had been responsible. The result was an open view up the valley and across the valley to the lower outposts of the highlands. That was enchanting. At the same time there was regret at the loss of the gnarled old trees.

Mason took the upper track at the fork, and found himself puffing as it went straight up the side of the hill. He stopped at an old seat which had been placed to catch the view through a gap in the trees when last he had been there. Now the view was broad. He sat for a few minutes, enjoying it, and running over the events of the day.

He wondered whether there was very much to this case. The deceased's notes for that review had been acerbic. Clearly he had been the sort of person who enjoys eviscerating someone else's work. If in addition he were as quick-tempered as Paton had indicated, then the chances were that there had been an altercation as the Scotts had described. It might have come to blows. In that case, if Emery were in a weak state of health—which would not necessarily be obvious either to him or to someone else—then a heart attack in the bath would be entirely possible. Raised blood pressure, a dodgy vascular system, anger, the shock of the blow, the further shock of hot water in the bath . . . yes, it all made a pattern. Find out who had struck the blow and then give the facts to the Crown: it would be up to them to decide what to make of it.

He whistled softly. Having someone else to decide what to make the charge or even whether to make a charge was a wise way to go about it. Yet he had been reading how much his English colleagues were distrustful of their new Crown Prosecution Service, which would do the same job for them. The fact that Scotland had had a system of Crown prosecution for centuries was quite irrelevant in their eyes. Stupid Anglos, he thought, and levered himself to his feet again. Unless the idea is theirs, they write it off.

Still, it would be a difficult charge to decide on, he thought, as he resumed his progress up the now steep track. The law was clear enough: you take your victim as you find him. Thump someone with a thin skull with the result that you kill him, and the offence is murder. But then in this case if it could be shown, as any reasonably competent defence lawyer would try to do, that the blow was struck in anger, then conviction on murder might become difficult. Juries had a way of doing justice even though the logic of the law was different. Then too—Mason stopped short and swivelled round to look at the view—what if the defence were that Emery, known to have a short fuse, had himself begun the thing? What if he had attacked and the other, whoever he might be, had simply defended himself? Self-defence is a defence.

He clicked his tongue. Self-defence. But self-defence is limited to what is reasonable in the circumstances. Still, a single blow, say, would hardly be ruled to be too much if Emery had attacked. He must find out more about Emery.

He started off up the hill again, and then stopped with another thought. What if the other were a woman? There

was no reason why that might not be. Yes, he would have
to find out more about Emery.

In the meantime, he had a walk to finish. So he briskly
mounted the last few yards to the wide path which went
round the base of the public part of the Knoll, and went
back into the grounds of the Monzie Hydro through the
gate at the upper northwesternmost corner of the estate.

He stood for a few minutes just inside the gate looking
down from that vantage-point, down the sloping field with
its horses and yellow tansies. The horses had moved down
the field and were as far away as when he had seen them
from the path below the field. From this elevation the clean
lines of Monzie with its two red sandstone church spires
were visible beyond the fields. It was beautiful, a slight heat
haze beginning to mask the detail in the valley. Mason
sighed. It was a pity he had to work on a day like this. The
afternoon would be better spent lying amid the heather
which he knew covered the slopes above him.

He set off down through the hotel grounds, and down the
long path between the tennis courts where guests were
perspiring in apparent enjoyment. He stopped just above
the courts, admiring once more the fine proportions of the
hotel, with its flag flying from the square, almost Italianate
central tower. Then he shrugged—work called.

8

Late that evening Colin Brown, going about his 'business',
took a blue Ford from the Church Street multi-storey car
park. He had identified it that afternoon as a hire car, and
the chances were that its current lawful user was slumbering
in the Olympus Hotel across the street. With practised ease
he slid a wire through the rubber seal round the door,
caught the locking knob, opened the door, shorted the
ignition and drove off, the thrill of success reminding him

of other thrills, other thrills for which he needed money.

Almost three hours later he returned the car. To him that touch 'proved' him superior to the ordinary herd. There was another reason also. He did not want the police to get interested in 'unlawful removals' from that site. Having a ready source of transport in the car park near his flat was too convenient to jeopardize it by ditching the car elsewhere.

One more night's work would keep him going for a week or two. It all depended on how prices moved. And there was that unexpected bonus: apart from the video-recorder, he had found a wad of twenties tucked away in the bottom drawer in the second house he had 'visited'. He was, of course, sorry about the distress his 'visit' might cause—the occupants of that house clearly had taste and discrimination —but they would, no doubt, be insured.

He sighed and let his mind drift. He had almost enough now to set himself up as a dealer. That would ease things for him. He would no longer have to take the risks of burglary. He shuddered slightly, imagining what it would be like to be locked in a police cell with no supply. Still, that risk would drop if his plans worked.

CHAPTER 3

MONDAY

1

On Sunday Mason had a day off. Crawford went back down to the Monzie Hydro to continue talking to guests who had been there the previous week. He had blenched slightly when at the end of the Saturday he had counted how many interviews there still were to go.

'Discipline,' said Mason. 'The disciplined approach. That's the best way. My old trainer used to say that solving crime was more a matter of taking statements than taking pains—but I've probably said that to you before.'

Crawford's expression indicated some familiarity with the adage.

On the Monday Mason had to stay in Greyhavens to give evidence at a trial which was due to start mid-morning. It was a series of housebreakings that he was particularly pleased to have been able to end. The accused had mainly gone for houses occupied by elderly people. He hadn't done any more damage than had been necessary, and had always run off if challenged. But he had worn a mask which in itself was scaring to old people, and the knowledge that there was someone about entering houses robbing folk like them had had an upsetting effect on pensioners in a number of the better-off residential areas of the city. As it happened, the accused changed his plea at the very last moment so Mason was not required, but he went into the court to see the final disposal of the matter. He also inspected the judge with more than usual interest. A friend had told him recently that 'My Lord' was a keen fellow-member of a national railway modelling society.

'My Lord' was also known to take a dim view of crime.

Counsel for the defence made much of the accused's lack of resort to violence.

'Are you seriously suggesting that I commend the prisoner?' the judge asked eventually.

Counsel, realizing he was on the brink of a precipice, retreated and swiftly brought his plea in mitigation of the sentence to an end.

The judge sniffed and looked carefully round the court before fixing the accused with a stare. The court went quiet.

'He's a loss to the acting profession,' whispered a voice in Mason's ear.

He turned. It was Irwin, chief crime reporter for the *Greyhavens Gazette.*

'I have listened to what has been said on your behalf,' said the judge in a voice which, though quiet, carried to the four corners of the court-room. 'In the discharge of my function I must have regard to the proper purposes of the criminal process, which include the punishment of crime. Your activities have put many in a state of fear and alarm, and even though you have now been caught, it remains that the elderly who have learned fear through you will fear lest there be others, others who may not be as "kind" as you in your nefarious deeds.' The judge's voice clearly surrounded the word 'kind' with inverted commas, and Mason saw Defence Counsel's head go down. 'Yet what has been said has some force.' Counsel's head came up. 'You will serve four years.' Counsel's head went down.

As the prisoner was taken away Irwin spoke again. 'I bet he wishes he could have made it penal servitude, or breaking stones at Peterhead.'

Mason shrugged, and made to pass by Irwin.

'Any comment on the result?' Irwin asked.

'Not even "no comment",' replied Mason, with a slight smile. 'I hear you're moving out of town.'

'Yes. Down to PenIron. Any progress on the Hughes case?'

'No comment again.'

'Ah well. At least you don't object to the Press trying to earn a crust. What's doing down at Monzie?'

Mason hid his surprise.

'Monzie?' he said blandly.

Irwin snorted. 'Well, well,' he said. He looked at his watch. 'They'll be opening the Golden Boy soon.'

Mason took him by the arm. 'Look, Irwin,' he said. 'You've still got a chance. Why don't you take it, and just go back to the *Gazette* and forget the bottle. Write something nice . . . about the summer or something like that. Life's not all the mucky side of things.'

Irwin looked straight at him. 'My, my. A copper who cares!'

'PenIron's a fine place,' said Mason. 'Why don't you dry out down there? There's some fine folk who could help.'

Irwin continued to look him in the eye for a few moments, then dropped his gaze and turned and left the court.

During their conversation there had been the usual shuffling as the court was prepared for the next case. Mason saw Alec Shepherd put his head in at the door on the other side of the room and then withdraw. The next case was a drug case. He made his way round the court. Alec Shepherd was outside chatting to a couple of his men.

'I heard,' said Shepherd as he approached. 'Four years. He's in a kind mood, is he?'

'I suppose four years is about right if he serves that,' said Mason. 'Trouble is, he'll get more off for good behaviour, and there's more than a risk he'll get out even earlier as he wasn't actually violent. We'll see.' He shrugged. 'Good luck. It's the same defence counsel, isn't it?'

Shepherd nodded.

'You'll be all right then. He's a buffoon.'

Shepherd made a face. 'I don't like it, really. We're missing the major link. Still, maybe this lot will get hit hard enough to be a real deterrent. Maybe he'll realize he let your one off too lightly and knock them for six.'

Mason nodded and clapped the other on the shoulder as he left. 'Let's hope so,' he said.

2

Back at the office the report on the Emery post-mortem had come in. Clipped to it was another envelope which Mason opened first. He smiled at the contents. Thoughtfully, Drew had got his assistant to take a series of photographs of the head prior to opening it up.

'I thought you might want this to show to folk,' said a note with the photos.

The report on the post-mortem was Drew's usual model of conciseness. The deceased was estimated to be in his early sixties, and in normal circumstances, judging by the condition of his arteries and liver, had not had too long to go in any case. There was some evidence of alcohol in the blood. Death was due to a cardiac arrest of massive proportions. This might have been contributed to by a physical attack if that was what had caused the extensive bruising on the left cheek of the deceased and which had cracked a cheekbone. On the other hand a fall against a suitable object, such as the arm of a chair, might have produced a similar effect. Drew noted that the type of chair he had seen in Room 126 would have caused a bruise entirely consistent with that on the body. The stomach contents were minor, indicating that the time of death had been some hours after the last meal. Presumably the heat of the bath had varied the onset and length of rigor mortis from its usual period. Stomach and bowel contents were being analysed.

To the foot of the report Drew had fixed a yellow memo sticker with a large red question mark on it. Mason peeled it off and stuck it on the front of the Emery file. He nodded, pleased with himself. The report was more or less as he had thought it would be. He had had its main lines in his mind on the Monzie Knoll on Saturday.

3

Late on Monday afternoon the results of the tests on various of Emery's organs came back. Drew looked at them and picked up the phone.

'Alan? Drew here. The tests have come back on Emery. There's nothing conclusive, but there are traces of something odd in the stomach contents. It might be useful to check up from his doctor whether he was under any particular medication.'

'All right. I'll get that seen to. And sometime too I'd like you to come round and talk about the Monzie Hydro. You and Felicity were there for a couple of weeks, weren't you?'

'Fifth Amendment,' laughed Drew.

'Doesn't apply here,' responded Mason. 'But seriously, with that bruise we have to look into things a bit more. If he was hit and had a heart condition that might be enough to ground a charge. You take your victim as you find him, according to the lawyers. A punch that wouldn't affect a normal person, but kills a weak one, is murder even if that wasn't the intention.'

'That's true,' said Drew slowly, running over what he had seen at the post-mortem.

'Depends whether there is any surrounding evidence of assault. If not, then it could get difficult. You may have seen something. You never can tell what might be lurking in your unconscious memory, just waiting to pop out when you talk to a skilled interrogator.' Mason chuckled.

'Skilled? You skilled! Don't make me laugh. Usually you can't even decide whether to pull toe- or fingernails first,' responded Drew with a laugh. 'If I'd thought I'd have you dissecting a lovely holiday and prowling round my memories, I'm not sure I wouldn't just have let them take Emery away like any other middle-aged infarction case.' Then his tone became businesslike. 'When would suit you?'

Mason checked his appointments. 'How about tomorrow —no, better make it Wednesday. I'll need to go down to the Monzie Hydro myself to see how things are going on the routine sweep.'

'Wednesday's no good. I've to go to Edinburgh.'

'Thursday?'

'Early afternoon would be all right.'

'How about lunch?'

'Business or pleasure?'

'Both, but I'll pick up the tab. I owe it to you for those photos—they'll be very useful. And in any case, your wallet won't have recovered from the holiday yet!'

So it was arranged.

CHAPTER 4

TUESDAY

1

Mason turned over irritably and hit the alarm clock just as it went off. Beside him Jane stretched.

'You didn't sleep well,' she said.

'I've been waiting for that thing to make its move for the last hour or so.' He turned over on to his back and stared up at the ceiling.

'I know,' she said with a smile in her voice. 'What's wrong?'

'I'm not sure. There's quite a lot going on one way or another and yet I've a feeling we're getting nowhere fast.'

'Getting nowhere fast, or fast getting nowhere?' She squealed as he grabbed a fold of fat. 'Pig.'

'Don't provoke me, woman. I've just got a feeling that something's looming up and I don't know what.'

'This Monzie business?'

'Perhaps.'

'You said last night it seemed simple enough. He fell and hit his face. Then later he got into a hot bath and had a heart attack.'

'I know.'

'Well? What's the problem?'

'It's maybe not that at all. It could be that garage matter over at Cranside. We don't seem to be getting anywhere there, though it had a promising start. And there's the Teal Inn trial coming up next month.'

'Will that be a real problem?'

'Perhaps. It depends.'

'Why didn't they schedule it this time round? It would save time, and you like old what's-his-name.'

'They're not quite ready yet. Though why that is I just don't know. We gave them a cast-iron case.'

'What about PenIron?'

'Irwin asked me about that yesterday at the sentencing.'

'And?'

'Nothing yet. It seems to be getting Ted Williams down. But it's not any of that. I've just got some kind of a hunch about the Monzie business. And what's more Drew has too.'

'Now that *is* serious.' Jane laughed. 'Two hunches can't be wrong!'

The second alarm went off.

'Confound! I'd better get going. I've to go back down to the Monzie this morning and interview someone who, I'm told, was in the Windsor set.'

'Have you really?'

''Fraid so.'

'Find out what she was really like, if you can.'

'Who?'

'Mrs Simpson. The stories are so varied, even now that she's dead.'

'Women!' snorted Mason, and headed for the shower.

2

It was a brilliant day. Crawford was driving, so they made good time down to Monzie. As they turned into the drive up to the Hydro, Mason looked at his watch. it was just after half past nine. They had been less than an hour on the road. 'Do you know the road distance from the office?' he asked. 'To here?' Crawford grinned. 'If you mean that we've got here too fast, I suppose I can't but plead guilty. But you're an accomplice.'

Mason scowled. 'Just remember in future,' he said, and Crawford saw that he was in earnest. Silently he brought their car to rest beside a yellow Triumph TR7 in the staff car park.

'Even if we'd been in that, that would be no excuse,' said Mason, pointing at the Triumph as he levered himself out of the car.

At the Hydro he went off to the Manager's office, while Crawford made his way down to the room that Paton had made available to the police. Later he would move up to another office on the ground floor for the interviews, but he had to have a word first with Inspector Paget just in case anything had come up either overnight or while they were making their way down from Greyhavens.

'Good trip?' asked Paton.

'Yes, if somewhat fast.'

Paton smiled wryly. 'It's all right if you're in a police car, I suppose.'

'Not really. That makes it worse, unless you've got to get somewhere in a hurry.'

'Or it's "Follow that car" time?'

'Quite. But that's a good line only for a film. It happens more rarely than anyone realizes.'

'Well, Mrs Murgatroyd will be waiting for you. She's

always one to be prepared well in advance for meeting any stranger. And a senior policeman . . .' Paton shrugged.

'That doesn't sound reassuring.'

'Oh, I don't mean anything bad or hostile. It's just that she's of that generation, a bit formal. And she still likes showing off.

'I hope she may be able to cast some light on your body.'

'I've been thinking a bit about that since you were last here, and asking about. You wanted to know about noise.' Paton hesitated.

'And?'

'I gather that there were some complaints—or comments, rather—from people in rooms on that corridor. The maid mentioned that a couple of people had said something to her.'

'I'll need to speak to her.'

'I suppose so. There is something else. One of the gardeners apparently interrupted a quarrel between two men, one of whom sounds like the late Dr Emery, at the bottom of the hotel grounds one day last week. But I don't think there's anything to that. Why, my own wife saw another quarrel, also last week. I think she said she saw it off the road to our house. You know it?'

'Yes. Very attractive site you've got. Not too far, and yet away from the work.'

'It's ideal for that.'

Mason made a note. 'We'll need to have a word with your wife, and the gardener and the maid. It may help to build up some sort of picture.'

'Oh, come now. I only mentioned what my wife saw because . . .'

'Because it just might be that Dr Emery was one of the men involved.'

'I'm sorry I mentioned it all, then. Do you know how he died?'

'Other than that it's something needing investigating—no. Now, I suppose I had better see your distinguished resident.'

'Distinguished? Oh yes. I told you about her connections. But that was decades back.'

'You should have seen my wife's reaction when I told her I was to be talking to someone who knew the Windsors. It's still like that old song ... you know about dancing with someone who had danced with someone and so on until the final partner was the Prince of Wales.'

'Yes, I know. We still get the occasional reporter from some of that end of the market, keen on a Duke of Windsor story.'

'Does she ever give an interview?'

'Standing instructions: we don't know what they're talking about.'

'That doesn't stop them, surely.'

'It rarely does. In that case it's: "Mrs Murgatroyd has instructed us to say that she does not talk to members of the Press." That's not how she puts it, but it is better to be polite.'

'But they must have tried other methods?'

'Oh yes. We've had quite a few come here for a week or so ostensibly on holiday but in practice to try to make friends. I remember once someone published a photo of her. But that's the extent of it. She's got all her wits about her. That's why it just might be that she's got something to say to you about Emery. For all that she gives out nothing about her past—that is, except to a select few—' Paton responded to Mason's grin—'she has a great interest in gossip. Makes me wonder what things must have been like when she was in that set.'

'I'll remember that. Thanks for the hint.'

3

Mason was not sure what he had expected. He had wondered if he had seen her when he and Jane had been at the Hydro, but in fact he did not recognize her. Mrs Murgatroyd turned out to be a bright-eyed, chunky sort of person, more than a little top heavy, and still proud of her legs. That at least is what he thought later.

'Come in.' A cool thin voice responded to his knock.

She was seated in a comfortable armchair at one side of a gas fire, which, to his surprise, was on. She saw his look and waved him to a chair on the other side of the fire.

'I don't know if I'll ever get used to your weather up here. But it's my home now, so I'll need to put up with it. It won't be for too much longer. I'm eighty-one now.'

'You don't look anything like that.'

'You mean I look as though I've trimmed ten years off the top?'

'No. No. Anything but. I'd not have taken you for a day over—' he paused—'sixty-three.'

'Hah! Suppose I told you I'm fifty-nine?'

Mason spread his hands and shrugged. The woman smiled, and suddenly, fleetingly, Mason glimpsed the girl she had been. Then she drew her lips together.

'Now, what can I do for you, Superintendent?'

'Perhaps I'm a reporter,' he ventured and was rewarded with a crack of laughter.

'No, young man. Those vermin I can spot at ten paces —it used to be half a mile. You're the policeman that nice Mr Paton said wanted to talk to me. Or I'm a Dutchman. Which I'm not.'

Mason conceded the point.

'I'm sorry to have to make your acquaintance in these circumstances,' he began.

She smiled. 'So am I, young man.'

'We are here officially. There was a death in the hotel last week, and there is some possibility that it may not be as simple as it looks.'

'How does it look?'

'Coronary.'

'Coronary. So that was what took Walter, was it?'

'Yes. We think so.'

She frowned. 'I'm sorry. He reminded me of someone I used to know.' Her face softened at the recollection, and again Mason saw a glimpse of the girl. 'Handsome man.'

'Emery?'

'No. That's what I just said. Emery reminded me of Peter.' She saw Mason's puzzlement. 'He reminded me of one of my husbands.' She leaned forward and stared intently at Mason. Then she relaxed back against the chair. 'My Peter was a handsome man. Walter could be . . . when he chose. Peter always was.'

'You found Emery, shall we say, changeable?'

'Moody. Moody. I know you're not supposed to speak evil of the dead, especially when they're still on top of the soil—funeral's not past, is it?'

Mason shook his head, as Mrs Murgatroyd went on.

'He was a moody so-and-so.' She straightened in her chair. 'Especially if he came back up here for his tea or a snort of whisky. He always had his tea before bed. No sugar, no milk. He said it helped him sleep. But if he was moody I gave him whisky, not tea. Not that moods ever affected his play. No, dear me, no. He was a cool customer with the cards. Clinical, even. A pleasure to play with. You tell me when and where the funeral is. I'll send a wreath.'

'I'll let you know what the arrangements are, if we get to know in time.'

'How wouldn't you?'

'Once the body's released it's up to the family. Sometimes they don't tell us.'

'Ha! Don't toy with me, young man. Walter had no family.'

'I'm not so sure about that.'

'He never said anything about family.' Her tone was doubtful.

'There was a marriage, but it ended some considerable time ago.'

She laughed a twisted laugh. 'So the old sod was married after all. I thought he was a bachelor.'

'There was a daughter as well.'

'So what? If the marriage was over, then they aren't family any longer.'

'We are attempting to contact them, and we have the local force down where he comes—came from—looking into matters.'

She tossed her head. Mason had the distinct impression that she was annoyed—not at him, but at the deceased. This was soon confirmed as he sat politely and waited for her to take up the conversation.

'He's the only one in that case. The only one.'

Mason glanced his question.

'The only one I've known who has managed to conceal a marriage from me.' She shook her head, wondering, and then dismissed the matter. 'Now, young man, how may I help you?'

'You have already helped me considerably.'

'How so?'

'It would seem that the late Dr Emery was (a) good at cards, (b) attractive in his own way, and (c) sparing about the information that he permitted to be known about himself.' Mason ticked the points off on his fingers.

'Have I told you all that?' She smiled.

'May I ask some formal questions?'

'Surely.'

'How long have you known the deceased?'

'My, my! Isn't that a jaded police line? I seem to have seen it in all the books I've read.'

Mason shrugged.

'Well, let me see. He must have been coming here in summer for some—what?—eight or nine years. Doubtless the hotel could tell you that. We started playing together the first time he was here.'

'How did that come about?'

She smiled broadly. 'Suppose I tell you that he was after my money?'

'Was he?'

'No, worse luck. It might have been fun if he had been. No. You know the main lounge downstairs?'

'I spent a holiday here myself with my family a year or so ago.'

'Ah! That's been troubling me. I thought I'd seen you before. It must have been then.' She paused. 'What was I saying?'

'How you met Dr Emery.'

'Ah yes. The main lounge. If you've been here, then you'll know that there are some of us play bridge there of an evening.'

Mason nodded.

'Usually it's some of us permanent guests, but every now and again, for one reason or another someone doesn't come down after dinner, or is away for a few days. If we need someone to make up a four, then we try to rope in someone else. There's often someone in the room reading, or just sitting, and they're quite glad to join us.'

'I'm sure they are.'

She flashed a swift glance at his bland tone.

'You don't play, do you?' It was a statement, not a question.

'Bridge bores me stiff.'

'Well, you're honest at least. No matter. That's how we started. He was my partner, and we got on right from the start. It was funny. Almost telepathic.' Her voice grew soft as memory worked. 'I've not often had such a rapport with a man—it was as if we didn't need signals. I knew what he had, and what he was going to do. And it seemed it was the same on his side of the table. We devastated them.'

'Then?'

'I remember it was the Tawneys we were playing. Never much liked either of them, but I'd never beaten them. They were good. They're both dead now. Motorway crash.' Again her voice faded.

'What about Emery?'

'Ah yes. That's why you're here. Not to listen to the maunderings of an old woman.'

Mason smiled in response to her piercing glance.

'Well, you've already gathered that I didn't get to know much about Walter's family situation. He was an excellent bridge-man. Instinctive, and with that added touch of the born gambler that can see an outside chance and make it happen. It's an art, you know, as much as that of Woody Herman.'

'I beg your pardon?'

'The clarinettist. Played when I was young. Those parties, my dear. Those parties.'

She fell quiet and got up out of her chair and went across to the window. The light made her hair into a halo round her head as she looked out. She followed the flight of a bird, and nodded as it disappeared. Then she shrugged and came back to Mason.

'Sometimes I watch the tennis from there. It reminds me of years past . . . You'd like some tea?' She asked but did not wait for an answer, and pressed the 'call button' beside the fireplace.

'I arranged it in advance,' she confided.

'I had heard that you moved in interesting circles in the 'thirties,' Mason said cautiously.

'Had you now?' She plunked herself down in her seat once more. 'Yes. Those were the days. Unreal days, but fun. Mind you, in my opinion it was the best thing that happened that he went. He wouldn't have taken Britain through the War. We'd all be singing the Horst Wessel song. And a place like this would be a rest-home for jaded bullies.'

'Where would you be?'

'Executed for saucing someone important,' she said blithely, waving a hand. 'I never could keep hold of my tongue. If there's something to be said, then I'll say it.'

'Would that apply to Dr Emery too?'

'Oh yes. That's why you're here, of course. I'm sorry. Rambling on like this.'

There came a knock at the door.

'You'd better be mother,' Mrs Murgatroyd said as the maid left. 'How do you like my china?'

Mason looked. He knew little about such matters, but there was an elegance and grace about the cups and saucers. The decoration appeared to be fuchsias, and was obviously handpainted.

'Very nice.'

She laughed at him. 'Fat lot you know. So I've caught you out as dishonest after all. You don't know anything about it.'

'No. I don't know china—but I like the look of this.'

'Get away with you, and pour me my tea.'

As he passed her cup she carried on. 'It's one of the privileges permanent guests have. We bring something of our own. This is my favourite tea service, or what's left of it. But there's more in store down in London. When we come to the end of this one I'll have them send up another set, similar but with irises.'

'You know your things that well?'

'Of course.'

'That'll be useful if they ever go missing. You'd be astonished how many people can't give a description of things that go missing in robberies.'

'That so? I never thought of things like that. Mind you, I've always liked nice things, and once seen, usually remembered.'

'What do you remember about Dr Emery?'

She sipped her cup reflectively, then put it down.

'He used to like this china too—but I told you about that.' She paused, lifted her cup again and turned it in her hand as she spoke. 'My impression is that he was a very clever man, but with something missing as well. My father made his money in the milling business, and he had an expression. You know in steam there's a device called the governor, based on two whirling balls that open a valve when the machine's going too fast? It lowers the pressure and the machine slows to a safe speed again.'

Mason nodded.

'Well, my father would say of someone: "He's lost the governor off his brain." It meant that in some respects the man, though clever, had little sense if he got worked up. It's quite different from being dumb. It's someone usually sensible who loses sense about something or other.'

'Emery was like that?'

'I just have a hunch that he's the kind that could go over the top. Sometimes he got things out of all proportion. He could be rude, you know.'

'To you?'

'Oh no. He wouldn't dare. But to others. I've seen it, but never when he knew I was there. That may help?'

'It ties in with several things we've heard.'

'Does it give you a murderer?'

'Who said anything about murder?'

'You wouldn't be here if there wasn't something funny going on. He died on Saturday. You said a coronary. This is Tuesday. Why ask questions of an old woman who was down in England on Saturday?'

'Friday night, Saturday morning. We're not quite sure. But yes. You're right. We're not entirely satisfied about what happened. There may have been an accident, or . . .' Mason shrugged.

'All right then. Don't play games with me. You're wondering whether he could've provoked someone so there was a scene or something, and the excitement killed him?'

Mason sat impassive.

'He could be rude. He could be cutting. He wasn't one of those who could quietly disembowel someone so they didn't notice—that's an art in itself. No. He was the kind that would be sure that whoever he trampled on knew all about it.'

'Sounds an unpleasant character.'

'Most of us are.'

'He more than most?'

'Perhaps. But he was a complex man. What you say about his being married makes a lot of sense to me now. Was there a divorce, a messy divorce?'

'I don't know about that. But there was a divorce.'

'Well, that may be why he was so bitter and could be so rude. But I noticed that if you stood up to him he was nice as ninepence.'

'So how does that help me?'

'It only happened if he was up against someone he thought his equal—I don't know if he thought anyone could be his superior. If an inferior crossed him, you could see his blood pressure rise.'

'So if an inferior had struck him . . .?'

'Is that what happened?'

'I'm putting a hypothetical case.'

'In a pig's eye you are. But yes. If someone he thought nothing of were to strike him, he would have been . . . been . . .' She searched for a word, and found it. 'Been Magnificently Annoyed.' The capitals were in her voice.

'Even if there were cause for what they did?'

'Especially if there were cause. He had a high opinion of himself. I'm sure he thought no one had the right to strike him, even his nanny.'

'His nanny?'

'I remember one conversation. We had had a good game one night, and I brought him back up here for a snort. The place is teetotal, but they turn a blind eye to some discreet tippling. And we spent an hour or so just talking about childhood. His was a generation later than mine, but there were some similarities.' Her eyes went moist. 'I remember we ended up singing together. Would you believe "Christopher Robin"? Yes. We sang "Christopher Robin". Strange man, Milne. Strange man.' Again memory claimed her.

Mason waited.

'So we sang "Christopher Robin",' she resumed. 'And some other songs. That's when he said to me that he was never spanked, even by his nanny. Pity. It might have done him some good.'

'How?'

'Well, he had this high opinion of himself. But it had gone, latterly at least, a bit . . . rancid. He had a fine line in sarcasm, but that can get a bit much when it's a steady stream. He could be very amusing, but in a "put down" kind of way. I suppose I was always glad when he left after his two weeks. It was a pleasure to look forward to him, and the bridge. But two weeks was enough. Quite enough.'

Mason could see she was tiring. He got to his feet.

'That's been very helpful to hear. It fills in quite a lot about Dr Emery I'm sure we would have taken a long time to gather together otherwise.'

She nodded.

'If there's anything else you recall that you think might be helpful, particularly about these last two weeks he was here, perhaps you could let us know. A message through the manager would get to me.'

'These last two weeks. There was something on his mind these last two weeks.' She looked up at Mason. 'I'll think about it,' she said. 'And let you know.'

CHAPTER 5

WEDNESDAY

'Where do you fancy going?' asked Drew as he came into Mason's office. 'If you're paying it's only right that you choose.'

'Did I say I'd pay?'

'Yes. It's small recompense for having my brains picked.'

'But probably more than it's worth, given the size of your brain,' returned Mason as he got up and came round his desk.

They settled on McLaren's, a clothes shop that had a small but excellent eatery on its top floor.

'What have you got for me?' asked Mason as they settled down with baked potatoes and salad.

'I'm not sure exactly,' replied Drew with his mouth full. 'There's little doubt that he died because his heart stopped. That does do for most folk, you know.' He smiled broadly. A woman sitting at the next table cast a startled glance at

Drew as he waved an amiable hand. 'It's *why* it stopped that's the intriguing question.'

Mason knew better than to try and truncate Drew's explanation, but he put a finger to his lips. Drew looked around and realized that he was talking louder than was necessary. He dropped his voice and bent over the table. The woman looked sidelong at him, and clearly would have liked to move nearer.

'There's a choice, really. That bruise on the side of his face certainly indicates an assault. The skin isn't broken, as it might well have been if there'd been a weapon of some description.'

'But you can't rule that out?'

'No. True. I can't. But on the law of averages I would have thought that a bruise of that size and shape was more likely to have been caused by a punch than a blow with something fist-sized. The fist has a certain amount of give in it, which an implement does not.' Drew put down his cutlery and demonstrated by bringing his right clenched fist hard into the palm of his left hand. Startled by the noise, the woman's head jerked round. Drew smiled benevolently at her before turning back to Mason.

'And?' Mason prompted.

'And therefore I think there may have been a punch involved. In any event, depending on how the blow was delivered, whether it was a proper punch or more like a slap, you might think of looking at the right palm of anyone you suspect. If they had longish nails there might be some contusion in the palm—reflex from the compression of the impact if it was a proper knuckle blow.'

'Anything else?'

'There was some intracranial hæmorrhage, but I don't think that would be the blow. It might be an undetected minor stroke, or the start of a big one. I'll get to that.'

Mason smiled as he gathered another forkful. 'I suppose

this rabbit food is what you people recommend?' he asked, giving himself time to assimilate the information.

'Depends.' Drew cast a critical eye over his colleague. 'In your case I would say, yes. Too much desk-driving. You need some time back on the pavement, and perhaps a better diet.'

'Thanks. I'll tell Jane you criticized her menus.'

'I said "perhaps".'

They both grinned. In fact Drew was always highly appreciative of the menu when he and Felicity were at the Masons' for dinner.

'Still, from what you're saying even if we inspect each and every right hand at the Hydro, the lack of nail prints wouldn't necessarily mean that someone hadn't hit Emery. Then what? You think that he was heading for heart trouble in any case?'

'Briefly, yes. He was due for trouble soon. It's a really classic instance. It's just like someone hitting somebody who's got a thin skull. Knock him down, crack his cranium —it's murder. The intrinsic weakness in the victim isn't an excuse. At least it wasn't the last time I looked at Gordon's *Criminal Law*.'

'No. That's right enough. If he had a heart condition, even unsuspected—we've still to get a report from his own doctor—and it was aggravated or triggered into collapse by an assault, then the charge is Murder. Though perhaps the prosecution might settle for a "Guilty" plea on something lesser like culpable homicide.'

'I suppose that's out of your hands?'

Mason nodded. 'Still, I'm impressed by your research since Monday.'

Drew looked his question.

'I seem to recall me telling you the Law on Monday.'

Drew laughed. 'Quite right. You're better than you look. I did have a look at the books.'

'They say that the easiest way to be cleverer than you look is to look a bit stupider than you are,' observed Mason placidly.

Drew ignored the comment. 'Might the charge depend on other circumstances? Say Emery had provoked the assault?'

'What makes you say that?'

'That's what's paying for the lunch.'

'How do you mean?'

'You said you wanted to probe my memory about the holiday at the Monzie Hydro, so I've been going over the events. It helped to pass the time on the train yesterday.'

'And?'

'And I'll get the coffees. How much sugar?'

When the coffees had been fetched, Drew returned to the question.

'I spent some time on the train running over the days. All in all, you know, though my memory is overall of a very pleasant and peaceable time, there were quite a few occasions or incidents of one kind or another. Mainly parents and children, or children and children.'

'Inter-Drew-cine struggles?'

Drew grinned. 'Sometimes.'

'What about Emery?'

'Well, when I did think back properly and systematically, I can recall seeing him altercating—if that is a word— having an altercation with someone at least twice.'

'Two persons or one person twice?'

'Two persons.'

'Who?'

'I don't know. Both guests, I suppose. One was a male in shorts. Might have been dressed for tennis, but it was on the higher road round to the golf course. You know it?'

'Yes. That could be anyone up there. It's a public road. Who was the other?'

'The other was a young woman—or youngish. It was earlier on the Friday, the middle Friday as it were.'

Mason got out his diary. 'And where was the other?'

'Down on the drive.'

'When?'

'That would have been on the Monday or the Tuesday of the second week.'

Mason checked. 'You mean the Tuesday?'

'I suppose so. Is it that important?'

'Perhaps. Sometimes the detail is important. Anything else on that?'

'I don't really think so.'

'Would you mind giving me this in the form of a statement later on?'

'I suppose not.' Drew's tone was, however, doubtful.

'You said something about stomach contents?'

'Mmm?'

'You asked if we could find out what medicines he was on to cross-check with the lab results on the gut.'

'Oh yes. I was coming to that. Sorry. I've been thinking too much of our own evidence, as it were.'

'Our?'

'Yeah. Felicity was with me when we saw the row on the upper road.'

'Good.'

'Now wait. I don't want Felicity drawn into anything.'

'I won't draw her into anything, unless . . .' Mason gestured, a pleading sort of gesture, palm turning out. As he did so the woman at the nearby table got up to leave. She looked carefully at the two of them as she passed.

'I'd love to know what's going through her mind,' laughed Mason as she disappeared.

Drew nodded. 'Still, I know what you mean about Felicity. If for some very good reason you do need evidence of that row, then she'll have to be included. But I hope not.'

'I'm pretty sure we won't need her. But you were saying about Emery?'

'Ah yes. His gut. There were some traces there. Now if he were on a heart or blood pressure drug that might explain it. But . . .'

'There was nothing of that nature among his effects.'

'Indeed.'

'No. There was just the usual. Soap, shaving cream, headache pills, deodorant. The only unusual thing was that the dental fixative was French.'

'Hmm.'

'Well, we'll need to see what his own doctor comes up with. Unfortunately he's gone on holiday apparently and the locum hasn't access to the full range of files—or so he says, according to the folk down there.'

'That's rubbish. Of course he's got access to the files. He just doesn't want to be bothered.'

'That's what I thought. In fact I thought further. I thought that it was perhaps the folk down there hadn't got along to ask at the surgery just yet.'

'If it were a secretary talking to a secretary, you might be fobbed off that way. But it could be important. It would be useful to have the information soon. Or even the notes themselves.'

'I'll get them requisitioned,' said Mason, looking quizzically at his friend.

Drew smiled. 'You might also see if you can find out what Emery had to eat and drink that evening.'

'Any special reason?'

'Yes,' said Drew seriously. 'We are having a thorough look at the contents of the gut, liver, kidneys and vascular system. There is just a chance that you're dealing with a poisoning.'

'Is there indeed,' said Mason slowly, with a frown.

'There is a class of drugs, the monoamine oxidase inhibitors, which can produce a severe hypertensive reaction, especially in someone already with such problems. I'm thinking of the phenelzine sulphates particularly. Cheddar cheese or broad beans or Chianti will interact with them with killing effects in severe cases. If Emery were on something like that he would have been warned to avoid them. If he were induced to ingest even quite a small amount of the drug, given his arteries and, I think, his existing hypertensive state, it would give him at least a severe headache. In a suitable physique there would be possible intracranial hæmorrhage or a heart attack.'

'I see.'

'So, if you can get that data from Emery's doctor, it might help me. In any event I'll let you know as soon as possible.'

Mason sat back. The tension that had grown round the table was released. By common though unspoken consent 'business' was over. Their conversation turned to other matters.

CHAPTER 6

THURSDAY

1

On the Thursday morning Alan Mason was getting on with the paperwork which had accumulated during his days down at the Monzie Hydro. Much of it was routine, but there was the occasional matter which required thought rather than a brief pencilled note on the bottom for the secretary to massage into formal police-ese. His phone rang. It was the Big Boss.

A couple of minutes later he went into the Chief Constable's office. The desk was clear, except for a white sheet of paper and a bulky buff gusset envelope. The Boss slid the envelope across to Mason but spoke before he could investigate its contents.

'You're dealing with that death down at Monzie, aren't you?'

Mason knew that this was a mere pretence of ignorance, but went with the gambit.

'Yes, sir.'

'Getting anywhere?'

'We're eliminating a lot of things, but it could be a longish job.'

The Boss grunted and tried to slide the letter across the desktop as well but air resistance halted it half way. Mason hesitated, then, in response to a gesture, leaned over and picked the letter up.

'It'll be a longish job indeed,' said the Boss drily. 'It'll have to be very thorough. Take that lot away and have a look. Marjorie will let you have copies of my replies later in the morning. Now, how's your laddie settling down?'

Mason's son, Eric, had recently taken a job down in London, and thanks to another investigation which required some London interviews, Mason had been down there recently. The two men spent a few minutes discussing their respective children before Mason was able to make his way back to his office and find out what he had been given.

He looked at the letter first.

It was from the Editor of the *New Inquirer*, a London weekly of some repute. Correctly addressed to the Chief Constable, with all his various decorations, the letter asked that the Editor be kept informed about progress made in the investigations of the death of the late Professor Emery,

who had died at the Monzie Hydro, Monzie, on the previous
Saturday. The Editor hoped that the death would be fully
investigated.

Mason turned to the buff envelope. It had been sent First
Class and by Recorded Delivery. He tipped it out on to his
desk. Inside were a number of other envelopes, some of
which had been opened. On each of the opened envelopes
a brief note and date in the Big Boss's hand indicated that
he had opened it. Each of the envelopes had a year indicated
on them in a flowing script which Mason did not recognize.
On one or two the single word 'Death' was added. Two
were marked 'Mutilation'. Several were designated 'Anatomically Unlikely'. Four, each of which the Big Boss had
opened, were inscribed in the same flowing hand: 'To Whom
It May Concern in the Event of My Death—' the words
'My Death' being underlined. One larger brown envelope,
also opened, was addressed to the Chief Officer of Police,
Greyhavens Police Station, Greyhavens. The postcode was
wrong, as was that on the bulky envelope which had contained them all.

The brown envelope contained a letter from a solicitor in
Bristol. Its pretentious prose intimated that the writer,
Gregory Cranford, of Messrs Nightingale, Cranford and
Buddle, the Sole Executor of Dr Walter Emery, Deceased,
3 Boulder Row, Cancaster, was acting in accordance with
instructions left by his late client. In terms of the Will, in
the event of the death of Walter Emery 'from any other than
the standard natural causes, and under anything but the
most unquestionable and regular circumstances' the writer
was required to forward the contents of the envelope to 'the
Chief Officer of Police for the County' in the case of death
in the United Kingdom, or to 'whoever might be the person
of equivalent rank in other cases' so that 'that person
may properly consider whether my decease may have been
brought about by the criminal intent of any of those mis-

guided fools who have failed to recognize truth when it was spoken or written.'

There had also been an instruction that the Executor should inform the Editor of the *New Inquirer* of the death. The solicitor himself did not understand what significance might lie in any of the instructions, but, 'gathering from a telephone conversation with the Manager of the Monzie Hydropathic Hotel that there was a police interest in the death of his client', he was complying with them. He would be pleased to have an official acknowledgement of receipt of his letter and of the contents of the envelope. He therefore enclosed a letter for signature, scheduling the material sent.

Eyebrows raised, Mason turned to the other envelopes, starting with the smallest of the four addressed 'To Whom It May Concern'. Its three sheets were written in the flowing hand that appeared on its envelope, and the letter was signed 'Walter Emery'. The date was nine and a half years previous. Mason scanned it quickly, and turned to the other 'To Whom It May Concern' letters. The next one he opened was dated nine months previously, the third twenty-two and a bit years before and the fourth seven years ago. He put the four in chronological order and read the earliest. Then he opened several of the year-dated letters taking them at random. He sighed, massaged the back of his neck, and resumed the 'To Whom' letters. After that he went through all the other letters, dating and noting with his own signature those which the Big Boss had not opened. Each envelope contained a variety of correspondence, but the bulk of them dealt one way or other with the Raven's column in the *New Inquirer*. Very few mentioned it in favourable terms. Clearly Emery had kept such letters and regularly deposited them with his lawyer. Some of the letters were handwritten, some were typed, and one or two very threatening letters were made up out of words or letters clipped from newspapers and stuck with glue on to plain paper.

Mason put the year-dated envelopes in chronological order—there were seventeen—and went down to the canteen for a coffee.

When he came back upstairs he sat and looked at the pile, sucked his teeth once or twice, and then re-read the 'To Whom' letters. He was just finishing the last of these when his phone rang. It was Crawford down at the Monzie Hydro.

'We're finished down here, sir. It's just a straightforward coronary.'

'It maybe isn't, and you're not.'

There was a pause on the other end of the line. Mason resumed. 'Something's come up. Bring the others back with you today, but we'll probably need to go down again tomorrow.'

'What's happened?'

'Just you wait! How long is it till Christmas?'

'Eh?'

'We've had an early delivery—maybe. But before you come, have a word with Paton, ask him what he made of Emery.'

'All right. We'll be in after lunch.'

'That'll do fine.'

2

'Well?' Mason came back into his office where Crawford had been going through the material from the envelopes. He threw the file he had been carrying on to a nearby chair, sat down and stuck his feet on the corner of his desk.

'I've never seen anything like this,' responded his assistant. He picked up a handful of paper and let it drop to the desktop.

'Careful,' chided Mason. 'We need to keep the years together.'

Crawford stuffed a couple of pieces of paper back from where they were seeking to escape.

'You've seen the letter from the *New Inquirer*? What did you make of it?' asked Mason.

'Difficult to say . . . I suppose at its worst it could be a sort of threat to stir things up if we don't do a good job on this one.'

'And at best?'

'At best it's notice that someone is watching us, someone who knows a bit more about the case than Joe Citizen.'

'Which?'

'Don't know.'

Mason took his feet off the desk. 'Neither do I, but when I was training my old boss used to say: "If in doubt take the long road round. It'll prove to be the shortest in the end."'

Crawford nodded—to an unprejudiced observer it might have been either sagely, or tinged with slight weariness at an oft-repeated saw.

'And in any event the CC says that it's to be a thorough job.'

'Ah!' That sort of instruction was more readily understood.

'So. Let me check off things to see if I've not got anything.' He went across to the window and spoke looking down at the car park below. It was raining. He raised his right thumb.

'One. We have Walter Emery, deceased. A middle-rank academic who feels that he has been thwarted in his career. We'll need to check out that end of things. I'll ask some folk up at the University, but I suppose we ought to get on to people in the South to check that out down there too.'

Crawford rummaged for one of the letters. 'He's got a gorgeous turn of phrase,' he said. 'I like this: "those fools who have seen fit out of envy and/or malice to have blighted my career by rumour, unjustified criticism, and otherwise poisoned the ears of those in whose gift proper recognition of my qualities might have lain." "And/or", that's a wonderful touch.'

'Yes. And there's worse than that. Still . . . Two.' Mason held up the index finger. 'For years this frustrated old man has managed to vent some of his spleen through operating as the Raven, the anonymous and savage reviewer of the *New Inquirer*. We'll need to find out more about that as well.

'Three.' Middle finger. 'Walter Emery was once married and had a daughter. Not surprisingly, given what else we now know, his wife succeeded in divorcing him for mental cruelty. He, of course, cannot understand that even yet. That most recent letter of the three shows that. But for some reason he also got the idea that she was wanting to have him killed. I suppose the shock of the divorce may explain that, if he did not see the tell-tale signs. And he lost the daughter.

'So, four.' Fourth finger. 'He started keeping track of things.

'Five. He had been writing as the Raven for a year or so before these letters we have began. The earliest of the threat letters was dated in what I suppose is his hand—we'll need to get specimens of his handwriting as well—the earliest of the threats comes about six months later after that letter about his wife's plots against him. I suppose if we check we may find that the style of his reviews had changed maybe, with the divorce.

'Six.' The thumb of the left hand was raised. 'Since then he has kept all the threats that came in to the *New Inquirer* and were sent on by them to him and he's deposited them with his lawyer with instructions to send them on in case they might help to solve his death.

'And therefore seven. We've got that heap to go through and eliminate.'

Mason swung back from the window. 'Well?' He raised his hands, palms out.

'Yeah. Agreed,' Crawford replied. He brushed his hand over the piled paper in front of him. 'I just wonder why the *Inquirer* sent on the threats to Emery. I'd have thought that they'd not have wanted to upset him if he was as touchy as he seems to have been. He sounds paranoid to me.'

It was Mason's turn to nod.

'And why he didn't get in touch with the police himself about them all?' puzzled Crawford.

'Maybe he did. We'll need to check his local force too. But in any case I bet it fed his warped ego,' replied Mason. 'To feel himself hated probably gave his life some meaning. I'll bet the same sort of thing applies to his feeling himself unjustly passed over in his ordinary work. He probably was academically nondescript, and didn't get on because no one noticed him. But it's much more satisfactory to feel that you've been done down than that you've simply not been noticed.'

He saw Crawford twitch a smile. 'Happens here too, does it?' he asked. There had been a set of promotions recently announced. 'You get on with those studies of yours. Paper qualifications can help.'

Crawford shrugged. 'I'd better tally off all these against the guest lists at the Hydro.'

'And in the other guest-houses and hotels in Monzie generally for the period.'

Crawford sighed.

Mason grinned. 'There's not all that many, really.'

'Forty-three names, fifty-seven letters,' came the swift reply.

Mason smiled broadly. 'You knew I'd ask that.' He clapped Crawford on the shoulder. 'You're coming on. But I've got some help for us. The CC has allocated another five to do the legwork.'

Crawford was surprised and showed it.

'Only for tomorrow,' explained Mason. 'Saturday is the usual change-over day at most of the hotels and guesthouses. We need to check tomorrow in case there is anyone interesting in the area—just in case they're leaving with a job well done.'

'But wouldn't they have left last weekend?'

'Perhaps. Perhaps not. The long way . . .' His voice tailed off as Crawford responded: 'May be the shortest in the end.'

'I'll list the names. Anything else?'

'I don't think so. I'll come down tomorrow as well.'

'What about Wessex?'

'I've arranged to go down and see the lawyer on Monday. He may know more than he says. I've also phoned Wessex University and I'll talk to Emery's boss down there, and whoever acted as his secretary. Usually the secretaries know a whole lot more than people think about the folk they work for. Then also there's anyone else that the local force may have turned up. It may take a couple of days. But in the meantime we've got quite a lot to do here.'

'Can't our people down there do all that sort of thing?'

Mason smiled. 'It's not a junket or freebie, if that's what you're thinking. Yes, the local force could do a lot, but often it's better to get whatever's going yourself. That way it's not filtered through other minds.'

Crawford nodded. 'I see. That way you don't get affected by their presuppositions.'

Mason looked surprised. 'I suppose that is what I mean. But I'm not sure I'd put it like that.'

Crawford waited.

'I suppose you're right,' said Mason eventually.

CHAPTER 7

THURSDAY NIGHT–FRIDAY

1

Late on Thursday night Daniel Guido di Sassella sat listening to the radio in the Reception of Monzie Hydro. Despite the music he could hear the rain outside battering on the glass awning which covered the entrance to the hotel. The heat of the previous four days had given way to thundery bursts, and the crackling on the radio showed that thunder itself was not far away.

Sassella yawned and gave his shoulders a shake. The rain was the one thing which he persistently regretted about leaving Italy, although that had been some five decades before. Still, his father had been right: the opportunities in the UK had been far greater than those of their north Italian village. And for some time recently, when he had made his biennial pilgrimage back 'home', he had found himself missing the rain. He shook his head. It was amazing what one could become accustomed to.

Come to that, there was this job as a prime example. Who would have thought that he would find himself in his latter years as a night porter? Imagine him going all night without sleep! But it brought in a few pounds, and was not too arduous. In fact he only did the two nights in the week, Sunday and Thursday, his good friend Barney taking the others. It was an arrangement which Barney himself had worked out, and the management had not minded.

Midnight came, and with it the usual brief burst of news.

Dan settled. He liked the stretch just past midnight, when the music was more to his taste—more of the 'fifties and less of the noise. But noise intruded. An insistent buzz.

He went over to the intercom. 130 was lit. He flicked the toggle.

'Porter here. Can I be of assistance?'

'Quick,' came a woman's voice. 'It's my husband. Please get a doctor. Quick. He's having an attack or something.'

Dan Sassella prided himself on his unflappability. In that at least, he felt, he was the equal of any native-born Brit. He had shown it under fire too. By concealing his origin and falsifying his age he had enlisted in the Highlanders at the outbreak of war, and, much to his father's gratification, he had killed not a few Germans through his ability to take things quietly, and systematically and accurately pick off the enemy. (To his relief he had never had to fight in Italy, though he shared his father's hatred of fascists as well.)

'Yes, ma'am,' he said. 'I'll see to that. Someone will be with you directly.'

He checked the room number on the intercom and phoned the Manager, who told him to get in touch with Dr Malcolm, 'just in case', while he went to see what was wrong. Dr Malcolm said he would be right along, and Dan settled again with the radio.

About ten minutes later, just as Dr Malcolm came into Reception to find out the room number, the intercom went off again. It was 136, but this time all that came through the speaker in reply to Dan's question was muffled stertorous breathing and then a croaked 'Help'.

Dr Malcolm heard that, and, as soon as Dan told him the room number, set off at a run for the lift.

'But that's not the one we phoned about,' Dan shouted after him. 'It's 130 that you were asked for.'

Malcolm checked briefly. 'OK,' he shouted over his

shoulder. 'I'll go there, but you get someone up to 136, and let me know.'

'Mr Paton's up at 130.'

'I'll send him, then.' Malcolm disappeared into the lift.

2

Both cases survived the night. The symptoms were the same, raised blood pressure and severe palpitations.

'Lucky they were both reasonably fit for their age,' Malcolm said to Paton, the Manager, as they watched the ambulance set off just after half past eight.

'Odd that two should have been struck in the same corridor, especially after the death in 126,' mused Paton.

Malcolm nodded. 'Well, they'll check them out at Greyhavens General.'

'Do they really need that?'

'Better safe than sorry.'

Paton nodded. 'It's worrying,' he said. 'I haven't heard anything about the 126 business. Maybe I should let the police know about what happened last night.'

'Oh, I don't know,' replied Malcolm. 'They doubtless have come up with nothing, but just haven't bothered to tell you.'

'No, I don't think that's true. There's still a couple of them interviewing guests. I'll speak to them when they arrive.'

'Perhaps that might be best.'

'You don't think it could be something in the kitchen?'

'Not a chance. If it were, you would have had more than two down with it.'

Paton nodded, clearly not quite convinced.

'We need to be seen to be doing something,' he said. 'I think I'll call the environmental health folk in and get them to check—just in case.'

'Please yourself. Doubtless they'll jump at the chance of a day in the country in this lovely weather.' Malcolm grinned as he hunched his shoulders against the drizzle and prepared to leave the protection of the hotel's glass canopy and go over to his car. 'I'll be up for the clinic at eleven-thirty. If there are any more upsets I'll let you know. But the only thing I expect will be Mrs Forbes once more.'

Paton smiled as he turned to go back into the Hydro. Mrs Forbes was a long-time resident, well-known for the range of symptoms she managed to acquire, none of which required drastic remedy but all of which needed care and attention.

He had just settled to the paperwork of the day when there came a call from the West Wing.

3

Back at Greyhavens the Friday morning was miserable. The rain had started there in the night and was steady, with intermittent extra squalls, as Mason and Crawford set off once more for Monzie. The usual pleasant drive through lovely views was a drab progress through curtains of rain. Indeed the memories of previous days made the weather seem worse.

Mason snorted as they slowed on coming up with yet another queue of slow-moving traffic. 'Takes all the pleasure out of motoring,' he commented.

'At least this lot are being sensible,' replied Crawford, who was at the wheel.

Just then the radio crackled into life. Some miles behind them there had been a pile-up.

'Just goes to show,' sniffed Crawford a little self-righteously.

'So. How many did you say? I've forgotten. Four or five?' Mason changed the subject.

A smile lurked at the edge of Crawford's mouth.

'Three,' he said. 'There's three names on the list of letter-writers that were in the Monzie last week. L. H. Gottman, W. Pattie and H. Crum. The last two should still be there. Gottman was among the lot that left on Saturday before Paget had put a stopper on people leaving.'

'Indeed.' Mason's tone was thoughtful. 'We'll need to look into that. And to get three interesting names out of the review list for Emery sounds to me well beyond statistical probability. We'll need to wait and see, though. They could have nothing to do with it at all.'

'But how would they know about Emery being there? Even if they were the writers involved in those reviews, wasn't the whole point that no one except the editor of the *Inquirer* knew who the Raven was?'

Mason sighed. 'Yes. From what I can gather that was part of the mystique.'

They drove on in silence, then Mason spoke again.

'They're not the only possibilities, you know. I've got someone going through the back numbers of the *Inquirer* at the Library. He's photocopying all the Raven reviews.'

Crawford lifted his hands from the wheel in a speaking gesture. Starting with the palms close together, in brief jumps he separated his hands. Then he dropped them back on the wheel as a corner loomed ahead. 'This thing's getting bigger and bigger every day,' he commented. 'Is it worth that? All right—there is that bale of letters and there are these people who might have some connection, but does it really justify the time to go through all the reviews?'

'We may also have to do a trawl through the Voters Roll for Monzie, and contact the publisher of every book that Emery damned, and the secretary of every organization that he flayed,' Mason went on.

Crawford grimaced. Mason smiled placidly. 'My instructions are to be thorough,' he said.

'In that case, won't we need to visit every house and

hostelry within a hundred miles to see if there's anyone there with a grudge against the fellow?' Crawford's tone was close to scathing.

'Ian, Ian.' Mason patted his arm. 'Relax. I'm kidding.' He paused and looked out at the passing fields, then added pensively, 'I think.' He worked himself upright. 'In any event there probably won't be too much to do today. I want to talk to Paton, the manager. He usually knows about who's in the hotel. We've got at least two names to work with. You go ahead and find out whether either of the two are authors. If so, you'd better abandon the matter until I'm around—as reasonably as you can. It could get tricky, of course. I wonder when suspicion might be said to fall in a case like this. Go over that boundary and anything that's said won't be led as evidence. Just establish whether they write books. If either of them do, then hold off. We'll find out later what they've written, and see if they are the Emery targets.'

'All right,' said Crawford. 'But merely being the author of a book that Emery has slashed can't be enough to fix suspicion, surely.'

'You know that. And I know that. But when a defence lawyer gets going . . .' Mason shrugged.

'The questioning rules are getting too strict. How can we do our job if we've always got one hand tied behind our back and the other on a short fetter?'

'You're not criticizing the Law, are you?' Mason's tone contained no reproof.

'Just these bleeding-heart do-gooders. There's even some of them on the Bench now.'

'Tut, tut. But you know the rules. And we daren't mess up a case on a technicality.'

'So you do think there's a case?'

'Wait and see, laddie. But I've got a hunch there is something here. So has Drew, and I've never known his thumbs to prick when there wasn't something wicked around.'

Crawford smiled. 'Have you seen any of the columns?'

'There's one in last week's issue. And there was that draft on the desk and the discards in the waste-paper bin. They're pretty vicious. I'd not like someone saying that sort of thing about anything I've sweated over.'

Crawford grinned. 'Maybe in that case justice might be best served if we were to go too far and made the evidence inadmissible.'

'I'll pretend I didn't hear that.'

But Crawford, stealing a glance at Mason, saw that there was again no rebuke in the words.

3

At the Monzie Hydro Paton was waiting and took Mason off to his office, while Crawford went to the room in the basement which the police had been given to use.

'I was wondering whether you could cast your mind back,' Mason began. 'Did you notice anything unusual happening with Emery—to him or around him? You said he had a quarrel or two, but had he made any complaints about anyone, for example?' It was a taciturn Paton who had led the way along the corridor, but Mason fell silent as Paton ushered him into the visitor's chair in his office and took his own seat at the other side of the desk. Paton looked very serious.

'I've got bad news, I'm afraid. Mrs Murgatroyd was taken ill during the night.'

'Oh dear,' said Mason. 'I do hope that the excitement hasn't been too much for her.'

'No. I don't think it's that that's caused it, but I wanted to warn you about that. Dr Malcolm says she's in quite a frail condition, though she is refusing to go to hospital. She wants to see you. She's quite insistent about it. Malcolm has agreed, but asked me to impress on you that she mustn't get too excited.'

'Why can't Malcolm himself tell me to be careful?' Mason's tone was bland.

Paton laughed shortly and explained. 'Nothing sinister about that. He's been called away up the Torrach to see about a pregnancy. From what he said as he left there's some fear of a miscarriage.'

Mason nodded. He remembered the Torrach valley lying to the north over the valley from the Knoll. There were a few houses up at its top beside the huge dam that had converted the end of the valley into a reservoir. Electricity Board houses, he thought. Or Water. A smile flitted over his face as he remembered the swallows they had seen up at the dam when he and the family had driven up. Or were they swifts? He couldn't remember. He did recall that Eric had argued the point and proved himself right later on when they got back to the hotel and he had checked the bird book. But for the life of him Mason could not remember whether Eric had thought they were swifts or swallows. He shook his head.

Paton was puzzled at the smile and then the head shake, but Mason did not explain.

'All right. Perhaps I had better see Mrs Murgatroyd, then. I'll be careful. Don't worry. I was rather taken with her.'

'I'll take you along. She's got a nurse with her.

Mason showed his surprise.

'An agency nurse,' explained Paton. 'She's got a standing arrangement that whenever she's ill we get in an agency nurse at her expense. It's one of the luxuries she can afford, and it helps us.'

'When was she taken ill?'

'Overnight. The maid found her when she went in with

her morning tea at about half past eight. If she'd found her sooner we could have sent her off to Greyhavens with the others.'

'Others?'

'Yes. We had two taken ill during the night. Same symptoms and Dr Malcolm felt they'd be best checked out at Greyhavens General. I'm hoping it's not something in the kitchen. But if it was it would likely have been much more widespread.'

'Mrs M's not the same?'

'She wouldn't go, and Malcolm's view was that shipping her off at her age would be worse for her. There's a nurse in Monzie who we've used for Mrs Murgatroyd several times. They get on well together. So we got her to come up.'

'I see. Well, perhaps I had better see her. But I'll be careful.'

As they went to Mrs Murgatroyd's room Mason remembered Drew's question.

'Do you stock Chianti here?'

'No. As a matter of fact we don't stock anything. We let people bring in bottles, but we haven't got a licence ourselves.' Paton was puzzled by the question.

'Of course. I had forgotten about that. But Emery could have brought in his own.' Mason frowned thoughtfully. 'What about cheese? Is Cheddar and the like freely available?'

'Yes. Of course. Several varieties of Cheddar.'

'Do you think you could find for me whoever it was that served Dr Emery on his last evening? That way we could check.'

'Yes. I can do that. Unless it is her day off.'

'Fine. That would be helpful.'

4

Propped on her pillows, Mrs Murgatroyd looked pale and weak.

'Young man,' she said once civilities were over, 'I'm owing you an apology.'

Mason waited while she gathered her strength.

'It was pleasant meeting you the other day. I wanted to see what kind of person you were before deciding what to say to you. Last night, when I thought that I might not make it to this morning, I realized that was wrong of me.'

'I am sure you had the best of motives, ma'am.'

A smile flickered over her face at the address. 'You see, I thought I would be able to tell you some other time. But it was wrong of me. You were looking for help. I know something. I did not tell.'

'Don't distress yourself. It can wait till you're stronger.'

'I would prefer to tell you now, briefly. Perhaps I will be able to say more later.'

'As you wish.'

'Walter Emery—there was something on his mind. Some things on his mind. He had made up his mind not to return again, and he told me so last week.'

'Did he say why?'

'I think he had met some people and had had a row. Not his usual sort of row. Something else. Something to do with his normal work.'

'Did he say who they were? How many there were?'

'I can't think clearly about that, I'm afraid. I usually remember conversations. But whatever hit me last night has scrambled my addled brain.' She smiled, a pale travesty of a smile. 'Will that be enough just now?'

'Yes. Yes. It's most interesting and it does tie in with other things we've got to know. Thank you.'

He got up and took her hand. 'I'll come back and see you when you're a bit better.'

She nodded and fell into a doze. The nurse got up and came over and looked at her.

'She'll be all right,' she said in reply to Mason's quizzical look.

'Look after her. There's not many like her left.'

5

Down at the room set aside for police use Mason found that Crawford had been busy. He had already established that two of the names on his list had absolutely nothing to do with writing. Both were retired gentlemen who had come to the hotel with their wives.

'Well, never mind,' observed Mason. 'At least we know they're excluded from our list, so that's some advance. What about the third, Gottman, was it? Presumably you've got his address. We'll need to get him checked out.'

'That gets interesting. L. H. Gottman turns out still to be here.' Crawford savoured his disclosure with an odd smile.

'Does he now,' said Mason. 'How does that come about —and how do you know?'

'As to knowing, I went up to Reception to check the address and to see whether there was anything of interest in the hotel billing—telephones and such-like. There's nothing odd in the billing, by the way. It went through on Visa, was checked with the computer and there was no problem.'

'And?'

'Gottman apparently phoned back on Sunday evening asking if there was any last-minute vacancy for this week at least. There was.'

'So what are you holding out on me?'

Crawford smiled. 'Not holding out.'

'So you've seen him as well as the others, and that avenue's blank as well.' Mason dropped into a chair.

'No. I haven't seen her.'

'Her?'

'Her. And she's a writer. Apparently the reason she gave for wanting to come back was that she had found roaming up on the hill was helping her work out her next novel. When she went home, inspiration had dried. So she's back. In fact it seems she's back up the hill now, looking for inspiration.'

'Is she indeed. Did you get a description?'

'Late twenties. Long black hair.'

Mason got up and went across to the window. It was still raining.

'If she finds that sort of weather inspiring, I don't think she writes the sort of books I would want to read,' he said, nodding at a passing squall. 'But I wonder if that means that she's one of the people that Emery argued with last week. Mrs Murgatroyd was quite definite about that. Emery had had some sort of upset. If this Gottman is a former victim of an Emery review, then maybe we're getting somewhere.'

'Maybe. Look at her full name.' Crawford passed Mason a registration card. Mason looked at it and started to laugh.

'Parents should be forbidden from inflicting that sort of thing on their children,' he said, passing it back.

'I suppose so,' replied Crawford. 'But if "Lucrezia Hermione Gottman" does indicate her ancestry, then perhaps there is a fiery character there capable of hitting Emery.'

'Poisoning would be more the style, wouldn't it? Speaking of which, how about some coffee?'

They adjourned to the coffee bar upstairs. As they finished, Paton appeared with an attractive young lady in tow. This turned out to be the student who had served Dr Emery his last meal. It had been salmon, and Emery had dismissed the cheese board as irrelevant after such fare.

6

That afternoon Mason and Crawford interviewed Lucrezia
Gottman. Mason had their room re-arranged so that he
could sit behind the desk, and cleared all the papers that
had piled up on it into a box.

'What's this all about?' she asked as she came gracefully
into the room.

'Please have a seat. We won't take very long,' said Mason.
'Something happened here last week and we are seeing as
many people as possible. I understand you were here last
week.'

Miss Gottman subsided on to a chair. There was a deep
calmness about her. She sat, classically but naturally—it
was no pose. Her hands were gracefully folded in her lap.
She looked quizzically first at Crawford and then at Mason.

Mason went round to the other side of the table. Crawford
took out his notebook, but slipped it away when he saw
Mason's slight shake of his head.

'This is a lovely place, isn't it,' said Mason. 'I was here
with the family a couple of years ago. We've always meant
to come back, but each year we've left it too late. It's very
popular, especially with families.'

'Yes. I gather that it has its regulars.'

'This is your first time at the Hydro?'

'Yes.'

'May I ask how you chose to come here?'

'I saw an advert and thought it looked the sort of place
I would like.'

'You didn't know anyone before?'

'No.'

'So how have you liked it? You've been here—what, two
weeks now, is it?'

'Actually I was here a week. Then I went away. But I
changed my mind. I phoned back on Sunday and asked if

there was any space this week, and there was a late cancellation which no one had taken up. So I came back.'

'Your first week must have been very good.'

'Yes. It was. Mostly. I got quite a lot of thinking done.'

'Thinking?'

She smiled. 'I'm planning a murder.'

The room went quiet.

'May I ask who you have in mind?' said Crawford diffidently.

She laughed, a throaty, smiling laugh and shook her head, her long black hair spilling over her shoulder. 'Oh, nothing that would interest you gentlemen, I trust. But tell me. What do you think of this for openers?'

She rose to her feet and pointed dramatically at the table in front of Mason. She tossed her head, sending her hair flying, then stood, head back, imperious. She looked quite eldritch. She spoke in measured tones.

'There was no doubt that Jason was dead. His head was pillowed in his hands on his otherwise empty and immaculate desk.'

She paused, then spoke again. 'The torso was under the window.' As she delivered the last sentence, she pivoted to point to the floor in front of the window, holding the position for a few seconds.

Again there was a silence in the room, which she dispelled by resuming her seat.

'Powerful stuff,' said Mason. 'I take it you write?'

'Somewhat,' she said with a sigh.

'Fiction?'

'Three novels, one published. And one crime story.'

'Published?'

'Yes.'

'I've always wanted to try crime writing,' said Mason meditatively, 'but it's finding the ideas that's difficult.'

'Surely that's no problem for someone in your position?'

'One has to be careful. There is such a thing as the Law of Defamation, you know. And the other thing that would scare me would be the reviewers,' said Mason with a shrug.

She spoke quietly. 'You just have to put up with them. Most books don't get reviewed, and they say that any publicity is better than none.'

'That sounds like experience talking.'

She gave a small, tight smile which failed to stick in place.

'Have you been reviewed?'

'Not all first crime novels get reviewed.'

'What about your novel? Was that reviewed?'

She went still, then nodded. 'One,' she said.

'Unsympathetic?'

She gazed down at her hands, now clasped in her lap.

'Did the Raven review you?' Mason asked gently.

There was no reply, but Crawford, side-on, saw her jaw muscles tense.

'Was he hard on your novel?' Mason spoke even more quietly. She sat, looking at Mason, suddenly like an animal hurt in a trap and conscious of the approach of the hunter.

'You wrote a letter objecting to some of the things in the review,' stated Mason.

She looked down at her hands, the fingers intertwined. Mason nodded to Crawford.

'Do you know who the Raven was?' asked Crawford.

She straightened and turned to look at him. Mason saw the marked effect of her gaze on Crawford.

'Was?' she asked in a rising tone.

'What my colleague is asking,' Mason intervened, 'is whether you happen to know the identity of your reviewer.'

'Yes.' The bleak reply was made to Crawford.

'Who?' asked Crawford in a similar tone.

She shook her head, but whether in denial or refusal was not apparent.

'I understand that the identity of the Raven is a secret,' said Mason quietly.

'Rumour has it that he is Dr Walter Emery of Wessex,' she said, speaking still to Crawford.

'Rumour?' Mason asked.

She turned to him. 'Wait. Your colleague—' the tone was biting—'used the past tense.'

'Walter Emery is dead. That is why we are here.'

She looked at Mason quietly and, wide-eyed, shook her head.

'You're joking,' she said, turning to Crawford.

'I'm afraid not,' he said solemnly. To both his and Mason's surprise her reaction was to laugh.

'That's ironic,' she said. 'Quite ironic.' Then, seeing their expressions, she explained. 'I misled you earlier. Somewhat. In working out a plot it helps to think of someone real— you can disguise all that later, but to kill . . . you need someone you want to kill to get it real. That introductory paragraph wasn't about some poor Jason or other. In my mind that head on the table was the Raven's.' At 'that' she stabbed a long index finger at a spot on the desk immediately in front of Mason. He jerked back instinctively, as if a severed head pillowed in hands had suddenly materialized in front of him. 'It always has been.'

Crawford began to laugh at the scene, a laugh which was hurriedly suppressed as Mason glared at him.

'And your view doesn't change now that you know your reviewer is in fact dead?' asked Mason.

She sighed and shrugged.

'What if someone assisted him on his way?' asked Mason.

'I could understand that,' she said.

'Did you know he was staying here?'

'I met him one day when I was out walking.'

'You knew him, then?'

'I was a student of his at Wessex,' she said with a touch of defiance, looking Mason in the eye.

'Did he recognize you?'

'No. He was never any good with faces, though he did remember names—selectively.'

'Did he remember your name?'

'He said not.'

'Did you believe him?'

'I'm not sure. He's—was—a devious sort of man.'

'And you said that there is a rumour that he was the Raven.'

She nodded.

'How did you hear the rumour?'

'I don't remember,' she said quickly. 'Gossip at some party or other, I think.'

'Did you challenge him when you met him?'

'Of course not—' again she spoke quickly. 'I told you I'd been a student of his. He could be so withering, so fast to twist whatever you said. I wouldn't want to expose myself to that . . .' Her voice tailed off and she looked from one to the other. A thought had struck. 'You don't think that I . . .?'

To Crawford's surprise, for he thought they were starting to get somewhere, Mason looked at his watch. 'I'm afraid I've another appointment shortly,' he said. 'We'll need to resume this conversation some other time. May I ask when do you leave here?'

'I've got two weeks. I'll be gone a week on Saturday. Unless I can get another cancellation.'

Mason got to his feet. 'You must like it here. I hope we will not need to take up much of your time, but there are one or two things you could perhaps help us with. In the meantime I must ask you to keep what has been said within these walls quite confidential.'

'No dice,' she said. 'If something's off the record you should have said that at the start.'

'You're not a reporter,' said Mason, surprised.

'Oh yes I am.'

'Who with?'

'No one just now. My uncle told me that if I wanted to write I should take some time off and do it. I did that and got my novel written—the published one. He also said I should get on the horse again after the Emery review. So I took time off again.'

'He sounds a sensible man.'

'He is. Maybe you know him. He's Harry Irwin of the *Greyhavens Gazette*.'

After Miss Gottman had left, Mason phoned his office at Greyhavens headquarters and dictated an angry telex to Wessex to chase up Emery's medical records. As they were passing through the lobby of the hotel, another call came through for Mason. It was from A. N. Drew. Traces of phenelzine sulphate had been found in Dr Emery. Mason asked Drew to arrange to have the two patients taken to Greyhavens General checked for the same substance, and also asked for Drew himself to come down and test Mrs Murgatroyd.

But Mason told Crawford none of this. For the present he wanted to mull things over himself and wait for the further results, if any.

7

'Why are you spinning her out?' asked Crawford as they swung out on to the main road.

'What makes you think I am?' replied Mason placidly. 'Watch that cyclist!

'His own fault,' said Crawford as he recovered complete

control after a nasty swerve. 'No lights on a night like this. Rain and twilight. Should we go back and book him?'

'I suspect that you've just given him as severe a warning as he's likely to need,' said Mason with a smile.

'What about the girl?' asked Crawford again.

'There's something not right about that girl,' said Mason. 'She's keeping something back. You'll recall that *she* told me that Emery was the Raven, despite all that business about the head. And she slipped a bit fast from the cool lady novelist to the highly tense and then from the misreviewed innocent to that "off the record" point.'

'Yes?'

'So if we give her a little more time before we get back to her, it'll be interesting to see what she says then.'

'I see. You're not just playing with her.'

'Perish the thought.' Mason took a deep breath. 'There's a saying, "The truth always tells twice."' Mason fell silent again.

After a little Crawford spoke slowly. 'So the point is that Gottman won't remember the detail of what she said to us.'

Mason nodded. 'She'll stew a bit, but with luck she won't think we're very interested. Then when we see her again, perhaps she'll be more forthcoming. Advertently or inadvertently.'

He pulled himself upright and leaned forward, peering out ahead. The rain and bad light were making driving difficult. 'I want to know how she knew who the Raven was. Whether she struck him. Whether she was sufficiently angry about his review of her book to kill,' he said.

Crawford glanced at his boss. There was a bleak determination in his words. His own lips twitched downwards. He hadn't heard Mason speak like that for some time. Usually it boded ill for someone.

His uneasiness transmitted to Mason, who sat back,

deliberately relaxing, stretching himself into the upright of the seat.

'There's something not right there. She's hiding something,' Mason repeated.

'I didn't think so. What she said hung together all right. Though I agree that her emotions did change about quickly. But women are like that.'

Mason cracked a smile. 'I'll tell WPC Hargreaves what you said.'

Crawford's head swung left.

'Watch the road, laddie,' said Mason. 'If you get us home in one piece I'll maybe change my mind. Do you know you're blushing?'

'I'm not,' came the hot reply.

Some miles passed in silence. Then Crawford said stiffly, 'Maureen got engaged last week. To a bank teller.' His tone indicated contempt.

'I'm sorry,' said Mason apologetically. 'That was clumsy of me. I didn't know.'

Crawford shrugged as best he could while driving. 'Luck of the game. And secretly I find I'm a bit relieved.'

Mason nodded. 'Sometimes these things are for the best.' He turned and gazed out of the left-hand window. 'Those must be the PenIron lights.'

'Nothing there?'

Mason smiled reflectively, and ignored the question. 'Sometimes these things are all for the best. And maybe you'll find that you're better friends with Maureen now.'

Crawford's reply might charitably have been thought to have been a grunt.

'Now that lassie back at the Hydro—despite what I said about my doubts. She's more the type for you.'

'A novelist?' Crawford was incredulous.

'You read books.'

'There's a world of difference.'

Mason smiled, blandly.

'So who's going to win the Test Match?' asked Crawford.

'You see?' said Mason. 'You do it too. We'll just watch and see whether she tries to change the subject the next time we see her. Or at least she may try to get off awkward ground as quickly as possible. But if she's in the business of making things up, she may have something cast-iron for us, some story she's worked out. Either way it'll be interesting.'

'You seem to have it in for her,' said Crawford, puzzled.

'I don't want you marrying someone about whom there's the least suspicion. And at present there is.'

'Come on, sir.' Crawford was irritated. 'I can ask to get off this case.'

'Indeed. Indeed.'

After another mile, Crawford offered an olive branch. 'She didn't tell us about her uncle, did she? Until she had to, that is.'

'I suppose that wasn't relevant. But we'll need to remember that. Irwin's not above using family as a source, I'm sure. Or maybe I'm wrong. He's an odd bloke.'

CHAPTER 8

SATURDAY

1

On Saturday Mason drove.

It was a good morning. As they turned up on to the dual carriageway high streaks of cloud in the sky like patterns on a beach at low tide were crossed by a vapour trail.

'Wonder what it's like up there,' mused Crawford.

Mason nodded. 'One thing's sure,' he said as a car swung out impatiently to overtake them. 'He doesn't have to bother with maniacs on the road.'

'I don't know,' said Crawford. 'What about all those near misses. And sometimes those Russian bears, the Tupolevs —model—model—what model are they?' He snapped his fingers once or twice.

'Don't ask me!'

'TU-95s, I think. They and the RAF Tornados get pretty close. Close enough to wave at each other.'

'Sometimes I wonder why you didn't go into the Air Force,' observed Mason. 'It seems to take all your spare time reading about planes.'

'It's a change from the other stuff.' Crawford was taking the police exams shortly.

'I suppose we all need our relaxations. That's better than certain other things.'

Crawford nodded agreement. 'I was talking to Bill Schwartz. It seems Alec Shepherd came close to a break-through but something went wrong on a stake-out. They just missed a hand-over in one of the lay-bys back there.'

'Alec was saying he had missed someone important in the last haul.'

'He used to have good information, but there's someone new on the go. He's heard about him, but knows nothing other than that he's moved into the area—someone from the South, apparently.'

'I've always thought we ought to have passport controls at the city boundary,' laughed Mason. 'That'd help.'

'Pity we have to spend our time on this one,' said Crawford quietly.

Mason looked at him. He avoided Mason's eyes.

'Go on,' prompted Mason.

'I know there's that stuff from the lawyer, and that the CC's interested, but this case's open and shut. The man had a heart attack in the bath. As the girl says, a lot of people were probably pleased, but that's all there is to it.'

'Wait and see, laddie,' responded Mason. 'Wait and see.'

2

At the Monzie Hydro Crawford was set to find the gardener who, according to Paget, had seen Emery in an angry confrontation with some man or other. But when speaking to a detective the man was more uncertain than he had been with the older, uniformed inspector.

'I can't rightly *swear* to it,' he said, shaking his head over the photograph of Emery which Crawford produced. 'There's some of these folk here can be very touchy, you know. Hoity-toity. It might've been him, or it might not, as I seen down there.'

'Down where exactly?' asked Crawford. 'Could we go down and you show me the scene? That might help you to remember.'

'I don't know as I could do that,' said the man. 'Rightly I shouldn't be talking to you just now. There's all this rose-bed to set to rights this morning and then there's the upper grass to cut this afternoon.' He indicated a bed of roses which to Crawford's eyes was immaculate.

'It looks in very good order to me,' he replied. 'I'm a novice in these matters. What has to be done?'

The gardener sniffed and looked sidelong at him. Then he relented. 'It looks all right from a distance, or if you don't know very much. But looky here.' He cradled a head of roses, turning them over in his hands. The base of each head was thick with greenfly. 'If I don't get that sprayed the flowering'll drop off later on. And there's all the dead-heading to be done.' He twisted off a head which Crawford thought was in full bloom. 'Look,' said the gardener, holding out what had become a handful of rose-petals. 'Catch them before the petals fall and the life starts to go into the hip, and a rose will bloom on and on without losing its strength. Leave them and . . .' He spat into the ground.

'I see,' said Crawford. 'I'll remember that. And it's obviously a job that takes time.'

'Time and pain,' said the gardener, lifting gnarled hands. 'Some of the best varieties have the worst thorns. Like people, happen.'

'You're not local, are you?' asked Crawford suddenly.

The man smiled, straightening his bent frame. 'Sometimes it comes out still. No. I'm from near Southampton. Came up on war service, and stayed. I'm a Wessex man, transplanted.'

'The man I'm asking you about came from down that way, I understand,' said Crawford slowly.

'Oh. And what's your interest in him? Isn't he the one that was found dead? Gave Rhona a right turn that did, finding him like that. Dead in his bath, wasn't it?'

'Yes, that's right. We've got to investigate these things and we're trying to fit together a picture of his last few days as best we can. If you could remember what you saw it would be most helpful.'

'I don't know. I'm not sure I remember anything about him.'

'But you said to Inspector Paget . . .'

'I was mistaken. Now that you've shown me that picture I'm sure it wasn't him.'

'Well, all right. If you do happen to remember, perhaps you would tell us. My name's Crawford, DC Crawford. Give me a phone at Greyhavens if I'm not about here.'

'All right,' said the man, and turned again to the roses as Crawford went off.

3

Meanwhile Mason paid his respects to Mrs Murgatroyd. She was much improved. He found her sitting up in bed and pleased to have a visitor. He pulled a chair close to her bed.

'Are you making any progress in your investigations?'

'Not really, I'm afraid. Part of the difficulty is that we don't really know what we are looking for, and that makes it hard to know what line of inquiry to pursue.'

'I've been thinking about that.'

'Indeed?'

She leaned forward and patted his hand. 'One thing I have never tired of is the way you people up here put things. You really mean: What has an old bat like me to say that might help you. And: Why didn't I tell you earlier.'

'Not at all,' Mason protested. 'Perhaps some other day you'll tell me something which will cast a completely new light on things, but I'm not here to ask you questions just now. I've come to see how you are. You really were quite ill, I understand.'

'Was I? It certainly felt like it, but none of these ninnies have said anything about it.'

'What did you feel, may I ask?'

She lay back on the pillows. 'It was odd. I've never felt like that—or at least not for years and years. And then only when I knew what I was doing.'

Mason raised his crooked eyebrow and she crowed a laugh.

'You look just like Maurice when you do that. He could do that trick. I practised for ages, but never a twitch.'

'Maurice?'

'Maurice. Dear Maurice. But he's dead now. In the war. He was quite a hero. You'd never have thought it. But then, you'd not have expected him not to be heroic either. He'd not have thought about it like that at all. A job to do, so he'd do it.'

'What happened?'

'A German machine-gun nest, I believe. D-day plus two. Funny how I remember things like that. But he was fun. It was a great shock to hear he had gone.'

He waited while she pursued a memory, and then came back to the present.

'But you're here also about Walter.'

'That's why I am at the hotel today, but it's not why I'm here.'

'He recognized someone. That's why he decided not to come back. He recognized someone.'

'Or someone recognized him? Would it possibly have been that way round?'

'No.' She was definite. 'No. It was the other way around. Something upset him. He wouldn't have cared about someone recognizing him. He recognized someone and that upset him.'

'Do you have any idea who it was. Male or female even?'

'No. I don't know that and it would be wrong to speculate. My gossipy mind might tangle things up for someone, and that would be . . . not the done thing.' She finished her sentence with a slight triumphant edge.

'Etiquette was very important when you were young?'

'Oh, indeed. There were such rules as to what could be said and not said and what could be admitted to and what was not mentioned.'

'Unspoken rules?'

'Of course. There were those awful books of etiquette. But those who wrote them showed merely by writing them that they didn't know what was what. What mattered was what certain people did—how they behaved.'

'The Prince?'

'Of course. And others.'

'Always there are rules,' he said softly to himself.

She heard it and glanced sharply at him. 'Rules are there for those who don't know by instinct what's right to do.'

'Did you?' he ventured.

'Of course,' she said with a gurgle, and then repented. 'No. of course I didn't. I had a lot to learn, but I learned it.'

'How would you assess Walter Emery?'

She thought about the question before replying. 'He was the kind who would know the rules. He'd have learned them thoroughly. But there was a part of him that would love to defy them.'

'And would he do so?'

'Only if he thought he could get away with it.'

'How would that happen? Could he make a new rule?'

'Great heavens, no. He wasn't that much of a personage. No. He was more the type that would be absolutely respectable as far as every one was concerned, but if he was across in the States, where no one knew him, he'd spend some time in the—the cat-houses.' She brought out the Americanism with an air of triumph.

'And if that came out back here?'

She shrugged. 'The ones that had the nous to carry that off would be in the cat-houses here.'

'You don't think he recognized a cat?'

'That's not important nowadays. No. There was someone else. I'm sure of it.'

Back downstairs Paton caught his eye and steered Mason into the office.

'I was wondering if you were finished with Emery's room now? We could do with putting it back into use. There's a couple of guests coming in on time for dinner. I would usually put them in one of those end rooms. It's a matter of the view. The wife always asks for a room at the end of either of those two corridors, and Emery's is the only one that is vacant.'

'Surely. I'll just have a last look round early this afternoon, if that's all right.'

'Of course. You'll not mind if we get the room straight before then?'

'No. By the way, I've just been seeing Mrs Murgatroyd again. She's improving a bit, but she's still quite weak.'

'Yes. I know.'

'She doesn't have any family she could go to for a while? No disrespect, but I'd have thought a relative's home might be better than a hotel for a full recovery.'

'No. There's nothing. She's got a couple of nephews, one of whom I have reason to know she's done quite a lot for, but neither of them would be placed to take her.'

'Pity. Still, you look after her. She's a treasure.'

4

After lunch Mason and Crawford went back up to Emery's room. Crawford looked out of the window at the view across the valley. Mason sat at the table Emery had typed at. He turned to survey the scene. There was nothing unusual. The covers were spread on the bed with towels neatly folded on its end. Everything had been dusted. There were the packs of tea, coffee, sugar and the cartons of milk on a saucer beside the Russell Hobbs kettle. But something was different.

Mason snapped his fingers. 'The picture's been changed,' he announced.

Crawford looked at it. 'Oh?'

'Yes. I'm sure it has. Come on. There's nothing else here.'

As they went down the stair Crawford saw Lucrezia Gottman setting off up the path between the tennis courts. Dressed in a red windcheater and black slacks, obviously she was on her way up the hill.

He pointed her out to Mason. 'She'll be away to hatch more plots, I suppose,' he laughed.

'Perhaps,' said Mason reflectively. He stopped and watched the neat figure disappear from sight. 'Tell you what. Give her twenty minutes and then go on after her. I want to go through the statements from the staff about Emery's behaviour. While I'm doing that, you see if you can find La Lucrezia and pump her. She may open out when it's not a formal interview. Watch your step, of course. Remember what she said about being a reporter. She's bound to catch on if you're too clumsy.'

'I'd prefer not,' replied Crawford.

Mason smiled, benignly. 'If your exams go OK, you'll make sergeant. You could support a wife on a sergeant's pay.' He laughed, and went briskly down the stairs.

'Remember what we want to know,' he threw over his shoulder.

5

Crawford did not find Lucrezia Gottman. She found him.

He had walked up past the self-catering cottages and came to the road that Drew would have known ran round to the small hotel golf course. There he paused to take his bearings. To his left the road ran along a wall which he thought must be the end of the hotel property. To his right the road went round a corner some yards away and then obviously downhill alongside an open field.

He felt rather foolish. Lucrezia Gottman had come up this way only minutes before, but there was no sign of her. Above him birch and larger beeches obscured the view. A path flanked by dense bracken went straight up among the trees. Another track went along the top of a field to his right. It looked muddy, as though it was regularly used by horses. He climbed up to it. Just at the corner there was conclusive proof that horses had passed recently. He looked along the track. There was no movement even away at the end of the field where the track seemed to go into a tunnel of trees. He looked up the hill track once more, and the longer he looked the steeper it appeared. And it was a warm day.

He got back down on to the road. Again there was no one to be seen. A blackbird began to sing. He walked along the grassy verge, and, as grown men will do when they fancy themselves unobserved, kicked a stone or two as he went.

About a hundred yards along the road he came to the end of the hotel land. The road curved right and the view up the valley opened up. He went on round the hill, marvelling at the views, until he came to the golf course, which he reckoned must be directly over the hill from the hotel. A couple were packing golf gear into their car.

'Lovely and quiet,' he greeted them. 'No one around.'

They waved assent, but he dropped any thought of asking if they had seen a black-haired girl.

The road now deteriorated into a track and rose, passing into the remains of a plantation of trees. Then it came out on a saddle between two hills. The path split, one branch continuing as if to run right round the twin hills, the other going up and to the right. This he took and found a seat set to look out at the view to the west. A path ran from the seat to the indicator at the top of the Knoll.

He sat for a while with his jacket open to cool off. Then he took it off, rolled up his sleeves and carried it under his arm as he walked the few hundred yards across the hilltop to the indicator on top of the Knoll. There he traced various of the names before taking a sheep-track roughly in the direction of Monzie. This took him round a small stand of Scots pines to the steep craggy part of the Knoll overlooking the village. Some yards to his right was a clump of birch.

Again the view was worth the effort, and he stood at the edge of the drop for some minutes.

'Lovely, isn't it,' she said, stepping forward from the birches.

He was taken by surprise. The red windcheater he had been looking for was replaced by a light blue short-sleeved blouse.

'I'm sorry. I didn't see you there,' he said.

She smiled. 'It's nice to see a policeman who may have some idea of beauty. Has your boss given you the afternoon off? Or is this your lunch-time?'

'I wish he had. But I'll need to go back shortly,' he said, looking at his watch. And added, 'It's a great view,' as he turned to it once more.

She came and stood beside him.

'I like it here,' she said. 'It's so peaceful.'

'A good place for planning murder?'

'A good place for a murder,' she said, pointing at the precipice in front of them. 'But yes, it's a good place to plan a murder too. The contrast of the peacefulness and the scurry of cars on the roads. There is so much going on out there. I saw some small birds harrying a crow or something just now. That's it, I think.' She pointed out into the void at a wheeling bird.

'Possibly a raven,' he said absent-mindedly, but then swiftly realized a constraint had dropped between them.

'Well, I had better get back down,' he said, reckoning that retreat was indicated. But then a yell escaped him. He slapped at his arm, where something had just bitten him.

'Let me look' she said. 'I hope it's not a gleg—a horse-fly.'

The squashed remains were not readily identifiable, but the horny abdomen indicated the worst.

'You'd better come with me,' she said briskly. 'I've got some anti-histamine cream in my room. Unless that's standard police issue?'

'It's not worth bothering about,' he said. 'But thanks for the offer.'

'Don't be stupid,' she said. 'If that thing's been feeding
on horses or cows, you may have a nasty boil in a day or so
if it's not dealt with soon. Come on.'

She turned on her heel, went back to the birches where
she picked up her windcheater, a notebook and a pencil,
and then indicated a track running along the top of the
precipice.

'Is this safe?' he asked.

'You're not some sort of cissy, are you? 'Fraid of heights?
I thought that would keep you out of the police.'

He laughed, shaking his head.

'I'll go first,' she said. 'If you're wearing slippy soles and
do fall, perhaps you'll have the decency to miss me on your
way past.' Her grin took the sting out of the words. She
slung the windcheater over her shoulder and set off, leading
him along the top of the drop and then down a steep earthy
track by its side. Further down, they entered the trees and
brackened region he remembered. Here various tracks ran
to right and left.

'There's more tracks here than I realized,' he said, catching up and walking with her.

'Yes. There's lots. Some are used by the pony-trekkers
and others just are nice to walk through. But I like to
get out on the top of the hill into the wind and the view.
Still, it's nice to burrow your way through here. I've
seen kids having great fun. It's best if you can't see over
the bracken.'

In her room his arm was swiftly dealt with. She sat him
down on a chair and disappeared into the bathroom. He
took the chance to look around, but there was not much to
see. A block of paper was on the dressing-table beside him,
but he did not dare open the cover. Beside it three sharp
pencils were neatly ranged. There were a couple of books
on the bedside table, too far away for him to read the titles,

but they were thick and the top cover looked glossy. He heard her opening and closing a bathroom cabinet.

'Do you want to cut it?' she asked, producing a razor blade. 'It might help get any poison out.'

He shook his head, and contented himself with squeezing the area. A drop of dark blood came out which she wiped with a tissue.

'You would be better to make sure that there's nothing left,' she said. 'I bet there's a chance you walloped the thing and got more into you than you think.'

'Perhaps,' he replied. 'But just put some of your magic cream on it, and that'll do.'

He watched her as she knelt beside him to attend to the bite.

'Girl Guide, were you?'

She smiled. 'Once upon a time.'

'And now you're a writer? You look like a writer.'

'Sort of. I'm just learning the trade.'

'I thought writers just wrote.'

She sat back on her heels and tossed her head to rearrange her hair. 'There's very few can do that. In the main it is a lot of hard work.'

'But don't you make it up as you go along?'

'Sometimes. But it does help to have some idea of where things are going. Some plot things out in great detail. Others start and see where they get to.'

'And you? You said you were here to plot a murder.'

She got up and sat on the end of the bed.

'That was a bit flippant, I suppose. I go that way when I'm frightened. But it's true. I am thinking out a murder mystery.'

'With a head on a table? Sounds more like a horror story.'

She shrugged. 'I don't know. I felt pretty murderous about it.'

She got up and went to the window. 'The review hurt. It

was what one would call fairly penetrating.' She turned abruptly back to the room. 'Enough of that. How does it feel?'

'OK, I think.' He flexed the muscles and twisted his arm backwards and forwards.

'You'll know by tonight,' she said. 'I still think you should have cut it.'

He stood there awkwardly. She did nothing to help.

'I'd better get back to work,' he said.

'Do you ever go off duty?' Her expressionless face left him uncertain how to take the question.

'We've still got a lot to do. It's difficult in a hotel with the changing population.'

'It must be.' She went to the door and opened it.

'Thanks for your help. I'll let you know if I come down with the plague.'

She avoided his eyes as he went out.

6

'Well?' said Mason when Crawford had tracked him down. 'What about La Lucrezia?'

'Not much to tell,' replied Crawford.

'Not very much,' Mason agreed shortly thereafter. 'What kind of feel did you get? What's her room like? Is it a novelist's room, or a murderess's?'

'Neither, really,' replied Crawford thoughtfully. 'It was kind of neat. There was some paper on the table, so I suppose she could be doing some writing. Yes. Now that I think of it, I suppose she must be. There were some pencils in a row beside the paper.'

'Maybe she sketches?'

'I don't know about that. She never said anything about that sort of thing. But the paper was one of those blocks with a blue cover. "Two Hundred Sheets" it said on the outside. It could have been drawing paper.'

'What size was it?'

'The usual writing size, I would say.'

'Not bigger? Drawing paper is usually bigger.'

'No.'

'Nothing in the waste-paper bin?'

'Not that I saw.'

'Did you look?'

'No.'

'Why not?'

'I was there for medical attention. If I'd started roaming around looking at things, she would have clammed up. She was getting anti-histamine from the bathroom. She might well have come back while I was prowling.'

'I suppose so. Still, what do you think? Any hunch?'

'She seems genuine enough. The only odd thing was that she suddenly shut down on me, like I said.'

'And you don't know what triggered that.' It was a statement, not a question.

'No.'

'But we know that Emery had reviewed her novel. And that she didn't like the review.'

Crawford nodded. 'Perhaps we should read that review.'

They went in silence out of the hotel into the brightness and heat of the late afternoon. Mason led the way round the West Wing and down the steep drive. They passed the modern indoor swimming pool. Shrieks of joy were coming from it as they passed.

'That's half the attraction on a day like this,' observed Mason.

They went past the open grassy area below the hotel. It was covered with families sprawled in the sun, grannies and grandfathers dozing, children racing about playing tag. A

few yards further on rhododendrons screened first the left
and then the right of the drive. The roadway turned steeply
to the right, straightened for about twenty yards and then
hairpinned to the left again. Mason came to a halt in the
middle of the straight section and looked about. On either
side the rhododendrons and some yew trees restricted both
view and breeze. It was hot and close. Crawford noticed
that the tar was bubbling in one or two places.

'Wait just here,' instructed Mason, and without a further
word took himself off into the rhododendrons to the right.
For a few seconds Crawford heard him rustling through
leaves and then there was silence.

Crawford stood, waiting. He felt himself begin to sweat.
Some midges began to take advantage. He swung his hand
irritably at them, but that seemed merely to call yet more
bloodsuckers to this new and enticing target. He waited.
Then Mason reappeared.

'Come with me,' he said.

Getting through the rhododendrons was awkward. Crawford was nearly poked in the eye once or twice. Mason
guided him to a low wall running down the hill behind the
bushes. Looking over the wall, Crawford saw a path running
straight up and down the hill. On the other side of the path
was a field.

'Over here,' said Mason, leading the way over the wall
to a spot on the path a little further down the hill. 'Now,
come and stand just here. I want you to see if you can see
me when I go back. Move about if you have to, but I
think this is the spot.' He pointed down at a cross roughly
scratched in the dirt of the path. 'And I want you to bend
your knees a bit. Imagine you're about five foot three. And
keep your ears open.'

Crawford waited again. This time waiting was more
pleasant, for out in the open there was the benefit of a breeze.
Again he heard Mason's progress through the bushes. To

his horror, a couple appeared at the upper end of the path. Feeling rather foolish, Crawford adopted a semi-crouch and looked back into the hotel grounds. With an ape-like gait he went a few steps up the hill and then down. Then he stopped on the cross. He could see Mason. Then he heard him. He could not make out what was being said, but there was no doubt that Mason was talking. Words seemed to be pouring out.

'Right, sir,' called Crawford, straightening up.

'Good afternoon,' he said to the couple who were now just upon him. He recognized them from the hotel. The woman looked somewhat askance at him. 'We're just checking something,' he explained, and got back over the wall. As he disappeared into the rhododendrons he was conscious of two pairs of disbelieving eyes following him.

'Well?' asked Mason.

'There's two very puzzled people back there,' said Crawford. 'But I could see you. And hear you were saying something. I couldn't make out the words.'

'Right,' said Mason. 'You're sure you could both see and hear me?'

'I heard that you were speaking. I couldn't hear what you were saying.'

'That's good enough. Let's go back.'

As they went up the drive once more, Mason explained.

'I showed a photograph of Emery to Mrs Paton this afternoon while you were with La Lucrezia. She remembered him. She remembered that Paton had said something about a fuss he had created a couple of weeks ago. More importantly, perhaps, she recalled seeing Emery arguing last week with a long-black-haired girl at just about where I was standing. Mrs Paton said she had been going up that path back there. It's a quick way between their house and the village when she doesn't want to take the car. She thinks the two she saw were arguing or quarrelling because of the tone of voice. But she couldn't hear the words. Indeed, I suspect she wouldn't have tried.'

'But she was interested enough to stop?' Crawford was sceptical.

'I think that's reasonable. After all, her husband is the Manager. She's bound to have an interest in any odd behaviour round the place.'

Crawford nodded reluctant assent to the point. 'I take it Mrs Paton's about five foot three,' he said.

'Sometimes, Sherlock, you amaze me.' The tone was teasing, then serious. 'I think there's little doubt it was Miss Gottman. So how does that fit in with your conversation with her?'

Crawford was about to reply when the yellow TR7 convertible came down the drive, forcing them to jump for the verge. The top was down. Lucrezia Gottman was in the passenger seat. She waved gaily as the car swept past.

'Who's she with?' Mason asked urgently.

'Don't know. But I've seen him around.'

'That's a new car,' mused Mason, looking at the corner where the car had vanished. They heard its throaty engine noise down the hill as it accelerated from the halt sign at the end of the hotel drive. 'I wonder if that's why she came back? A new boyfriend.' He turned to Crawford. 'You better get busy, lad, if you're not going to lose her.'

Crawford's expression showed what he thought of the remark, but Mason had turned and was walking on up the drive.

7

Back at their headquarters room in the hotel they found Paget. He had a satisfied look on his round face, his small moustache bristling with pleasure.

'I deduce,' said Mason as soon as he saw him, 'that you've got news for me.'

Paget nodded. 'I must say,' he began, rising to his feet, 'that at first I thought you had cast your net rather wide asking us to go round the guest-houses with that list of names. However—' he stood straighter—'I'm pleased to be able to say that we've found one of the names.'

'Ah!' Mason glanced at Crawford, but Crawford had clearly taken the point, so Mason did not rub it in. 'Which? Or who, I suppose?'

'Clarence Berman.'

'I suppose if I were omniscient I'd remember all about him. But I'm not, and don't.'

'He's a name on that list Detective-Constable Crawford gave me to have checked. He's staying in The Stable. It's a guest-house on the south road. No one has spoken to him, but the woman there is quite clear about him. He's been there a week.'

'Have you got a phone number for the place?' Mason asked.

'Of course.' The reply was reproachful.

'Well, we'd better check this one out too,' Mason said to Crawford, holding out his hand for the phone number.

Half an hour later Crawford drew the car into the gravelled parking area in front of a long building, which clearly owed its name to its former use.

'Remember. Don't scare him' said Mason as they got out of the car.

Inside they were met by a woman in her late forties who left them waiting in the hall while she went to find their quarry. Then, introductions over, she showed them into what was clearly a television lounge at the front of the building overlooking the car park.

'You'll be all right in there,' she said. 'No one usually uses this room before dinner.'

'Thanks,' said Mason.

Clarence Berman was a middle-aged man. At a distance one might have said he was stocky, but close-up he was above average size. It was his build which misled. His face was square, and there was an accident scar across the middle of his forehead which accentuated the breadth of his brow.

'It's good of you to see us at this short notice,' said Mason as they settled into uncomfortable armchairs.

'I don't quite understand what you want to see me in particular about,' said Berman, attempting to balance a whisky on the arm of the chair. He saw Mason looking at the glass. 'I'm, sorry,' he said. 'Can I get you one? There's a sort of bar through there.'

'That's kind of you,' replied Mason, 'but we are on duty.'

Berman sat back and waited.

'We are in the district carrying out some investigations,' said Crawford as arranged. 'We were wondering how it came to be that you are in the area.'

Berman's knuckles whitened round the glass. He raised it and sipped before replying.

'That is a long story.'

'We are patient men.'

Berman swirled the amber fluid round the glass and said nothing.

Mason leaned forward into his line of sight.

'Are you Clarence Berman, the writer?'

Berman glanced up, and resumed playing with the glass.

'The novelist?' asked Crawford.

'Suppose that I am?'

'Then you may be able to help us.'

'I got an odd letter.'

'I beg your pardon?'

'You asked how I came to be in the area, and I'm telling you. I got an odd letter.'

'What did it say?'

'Not much.'

'But it brought you here?' Crawford's tone was incredulous and Mason shot him a warning look. Berman did not notice. He swirled the glass another couple of times, then drained it.

'Excuse me,' he said and got up. 'Must get a refill.' He went out quickly.

Crawford rose to his feet, then subsided as Mason shook his head. When Berman had gone Mason said, 'It's all right. He'll be back, and in any event—' he turned in his seat and pointed at the car park—'you'd be able to get him if he appears out there.'

They waited, and Berman did come back, his glass filled.

'Now,' he said as he sat down. 'You were saying?'

'You were saying you had got a letter,' said Mason smoothly.

'Ah yes.' Berman studied his glass and then took a large pull at it. 'The letter.'

They waited.

'About three to four weeks ago I got a letter. Forwarded from my publishers. Marked "Personal and Private" So, very properly, they didn't open it but sent it on to me. They wanted to know its general contents, of course—most publishers want to know about reactions to one's work—scared of libel actions, I think.' He fell silent.

'And?' Crawford prodded.

'It was an odd letter. Said that someone I had wanted to meet was in the area.' He stopped and looked first at Mason and then at Crawford with a dawning realization. 'I say, that's not why you're here is it?'

Mason made a non-committal gesture. 'That's not important. Just carry on, please, in your own way. I'll explain later.'

This time Berman gulped at the whisky. 'It—the letter, that is—said that someone I wanted to meet was here.'

'Here? At this hotel?'

'No. This was the only place I was able to get into. I just drove up and then booked at the local tourist office.'

'And did you get to meet this person you were seeking?'

'As a matter of fact, no. I did not. When I got in touch with where he was staying I was told he was no longer in residence.'

'So why are you still here?' asked Crawford.

Berman looked at Crawford as at a simple child. 'I had to book a week, and that expires tomorrow.'

'You couldn't cancel?'

'No. I paid in advance. Besides, it is so beautiful here, I found. There's some lovely walks down by the river.'

'May I ask who it was you hoped to see?' Mason's tone was gentle.

'Someone called Walter Emery—I don't suppose you've heard of him.'

'And will you be able to see him elsewhere?'

'I dare say. I now know where he lives and will try to get in touch.'

'This letter. You wouldn't by any chance have it with you?'

'As a matter of fact, I have. Would you like to see it?'

'Indeed. It sounds most mysterious.'

'Just a minute.' Berman downed the rest of the glass and got to his feet. 'I'll get it.'

Crawford watched him go out of the room with some admiration. 'That's some capacity,' he said as the door shut.

Berman soon returned, and the effect of the whisky began to be seen as he leaned forward to give an envelope to Mason.

'Here you are,' he said, and abruptly sat down.

Mason looked at the envelope. It was double-franked and addressed to 'Clarence Berman, Esq.,' c/o a well-known publisher and marked 'Personal and Private'. The name and address of the publisher had been scored through and another address in Yorkshire written beside it. It had been sent through the post two days after its first franking. Both postmarks were in London. The later postmark was three weeks ago.

'Your publishers forwarded it unopened?' Mason asked as he took a sheet of paper from inside the envelope.

'Yes. They do that. I told you that already.'

The content was an unsigned typewritten note: 'You may be interested to know that the Raven is a Walter Emery who will be staying at the Hydro, Monzie, Scotland, in July.'

Mason read this and passed it over to Crawford.

'Do you know who sent this?' he asked Berman.

'No. I do not.'

'But you came anyway. All the way from Yorkshire, it would seem.'

Berman shrugged.

'But you delayed your coming and when you tried to make contact Emery was no longer here.'

'That is true.'

'But you were given his address—by the hotel, I presume?'

'Well—um. Yes.'

'You hesitate?'

'Actually—' Berman sat forward and became confidential—'actually what happened was that I went to the Hydro and they wouldn't tell me anything other than that he was no longer there. There was a silly girl behind the desk. So I said that I'd had a letter from him saying he hoped we'd meet, and that having missed him I was going to write but couldn't remember if it was "Emery" or "Emory". And when she looked up the Register I saw the address. I'm quite good at reading upside down. I learned to do that as a child. It's a very useful accomplishment.'

He sat back, self-satisfaction oozing from him.

'So you came here last what? Saturday, was it?'

'Sunday actually.'

'You said your publishers had asked about the letter?'

'Did I? Oh yes. Silly of me. I see how your mind is working. Yes, the letter was readdressed and sent on. My editor was in touch later about something else and mentioned that she had sent on a letter. She "hoped it was nothing serious". But I knew what that meant.'

'What does the letter mean by "the Raven is Walter Emery"?'

'My dear fellow. The Raven is a columnist and the main reviewer for the *New Inquirer*.' Berman's tone showed his opinion of those who did not know this important fact of life.

'And that is important?'

'Of course. The Raven is anonymous. That allows him to be quite fearless in what he says. In these last few years he has made many novelists. His recognition is a feather in one's cap.'

'I take it he liked your writing?'

'Quite so.'

'So you wanted to see the Raven to thank him?'

'Yes. And I wanted to see who he was. You see, his identity is not widely known.'

'I see. That's very helpful of you, Mr Berman. Very helpful indeed.' Mason got to his feet. Berman sat looking up at him, as if uncertain of his legs.

'I wonder if I might keep this letter for a few days,' Mason asked. 'Mr Crawford will give you a receipt.'

'Yes. All right. But I must have it back.' Berman got up

and staggered slightly. 'Oops. Just as well I'm not driving, what?'

'That's kind of you.' Mason gestured to Crawford, who quickly wrote out a receipt on a spare leaf and tore it out of his notebook.

8

'Was that helpful?' asked Crawford on their way back to the Hydro.

'Yes. I'm not sure how, but yes, it was. Mr Berman had a high opinion of our late friend.'

'Only because it was a good review.'

'But it shows that not everything Emery wrote was damning. There may be more to him that I had been thinking.'

'What about the letter?'

'Have a look.' Mason fished the letter out of his breast pocket and gave it to his passenger. 'See? It's an electric typewriter, probably using a Brougham type, but it's throwing a bit oddly. It might be a proportional spacing daisy-wheel on a standard machine.'

'So you think we might track it?'

'Possibly. There's also this. Someone's sent a letter to Berman with the "Emery is the Raven" data. I want to know if someone was trying to set a pack on Emery, and if so, why. I want to know if your girlfriend got one too. In which case she's been playing games with us.'

'She's not my girlfriend,' was the short reply.

Back at the Hydro everything was neat, and virtually deserted. Plainly almost everyone was at dinner.

'Good idea,' said Mason surveying their room. 'Time we were away too.'

*

'That's it,' said Mason as a yellow sports-car passed going south on the other side of the dual carriageway as they came down the approach into Greyhavens. 'Two in it still. I wonder where they've been.'

There was nothing on his desk that couldn't wait, so Mason went off home. He tried the radio, but there was nothing listenable to, so he turned to the police band. The chatter of the small incidents and minor dramas of city life was reassuring. There was a call for a computer check on a car from the north side of town. Someone had phoned in a complaint about a noisy party. An ambulance was called for—an assault in an office car park in the middle of town, it seemed. There was a drunk down near the railway station trying to flag down cars. Then the officer at the car park came through again. It seemed that the casualty was a Colin Brown, whom he knew Chief Inspector Shepherd was wanting to interview. The officer asked Control to inform the Superintendent. He thought Brown would be in Greyhavens General—probably for some time.

The name meant nothing to Mason. He turned into his drive and switched off.

CHAPTER 9

MONDAY

1

On the Sunday night Mason took the train down to Stirling and then the sleeper to Bristol. While leisurely breakfasting at Temple Meads Station he glanced through the local paper. Apparently Wessex University was, like others, having financial difficulties and was reducing its staffing. Then he strolled to the main police station for nine o'clock, where he met his local colleagues. They had made some inquiries on his behalf. He listened, made notes, collected a car, a street map and the Ordnance Survey map for the region and went to see Emery's lawyer.

Nightingale, Cranford and Buddle was housed in a downtown Victorian building and he had difficulty finding a place to park, eventually having to use a multi-storey car park two blocks away. The gyrations within confused him. Though he was usually proud of his sense of direction, he got turned round in the building, came out on the wrong side and walked the wrong way for a little before realizing his mistake. Feeling very sheepish, he retraced his steps and just made it to the offices in time for his appointment. He asked for Mr Cranford, and was shown into a booklined office, where an elderly man sat behind a mahogany desk.

'It was a most unusual set of instructions,' the lawyer readily agreed. 'But then our client was a most unusual man. Most unusual.' He shook his bald head.

Mason raised his eyebrows and nodded, as if slightly doubtful of the point. 'I am afraid we do not know very much about your client,' he said. 'Could you—' he gestured —'elaborate?'

'I really shouldn't . . . matter of confidence, really. But then I suppose you are the police and I think I am at liberty to take Emery's instructions to me to send on those envelopes as implying an instruction to cooperate in any way I can.' The old lawyer still seemed doubtful of the ethics, but the twinkle in his eye showed Mason that he would welcome some help in circumventing his conscience.

'I'm sure he would approve,' Mason said smoothly. 'Can I ask whether he was a longstanding client of this firm?'

'Yes and no. We acted for him—I acted for him—years back. He came to us through one of the estate agent firms to whom we are linked. Then he went somewhere else for a period. We didn't know. It was when he came back to me with the first of those envelopes I sent on, I think. He said he had been let down by his current lawyers—some argument with a neighbour about overhanging tree branches, if I recall correctly—and that we must be better lawyers than he had realized.' The old man began to laugh and for a moment lost his breath. 'Often happens when clients go away for any reason. They come back to us sooner than later.'

'You said Emery was an unusual man?'

'So I did. Indiscreet of me to say that. But then you are here in an official capacity.'

'I am here in an official capacity, and it would immeasurably help me in my investigations if you could tell me something about your late client. Perhaps things that I might not otherwise come to know.'

The old lawyer sat slumped behind his desk, looking with narrowed eyes at Mason, making up his mind. At last he nodded.

'He was an unusual man. Traces of great ability, I suppose, but with immense flaws. Might have risen to the top of his profession, but the flaws made him stick short of it—short by quite some way.'

'What sort of flaws?'

'You know that he was academic?'

Mason nodded.

'I sometimes wonder if I should have been an academic too,' said the old man meditatively. 'But practice has brought its own rewards. Still, Emery. He failed to publish. In his line of country that was fatal. To get to the top you have to publish. Doesn't mean what's published is any good, according to Emery. Looking at some of the things I see on the shelves, I agree with him. Volume is more important than proof—which reminds me. Would you like a drink?'

'No, thank you,' said Mason, surprised.

The old man laughed a wheezy laugh. 'I'm not offering strong liquor,' he said. 'But I'm sure you would regret your decision if you sat over there watching me with my tea. I always have tea about now.' He got up and leaned over to one side of his desk where there was an antiquated office intercom and flicked a switch.

'Yes, Mr Cranford?' came a voice.

'Tea for two, please, Muriel.'

'Yes, Mr Cranford.'

'We were saying?' he said as he resumed his seat.

'About Emery not publishing . . .'

'Ah yes. His trouble was that while much of what he said was good, very good—I'm an amateur in the best sense, and I know good writing when I see it—there were always bits that just were unpublishable. Libel mostly. And a fair amount of sheer scurrility.'

'Did he let you see the material?'

'Yes. That's how I know. We met at the golf club occasionally. I was able to get around in those days, and he was a newcomer. I remember recognizing him from having dealt with his house purchase some time before. I asked what he was doing with himself. He made some comment about the imbecilities of publishers publishing mediocrity and the way they treat major scholarly contributions. It went from there.'

Mason raised an eyebrow quizzically.

'He asked me about libel law. His publisher was fussing. I said for him to let me see what was complained about by his putative publisher. He brought it in the next day.' He fell silent, chasing memory.

After a while he went on. 'The publisher was quite right. There would have been a case about it, and he would have had to withdraw the book. Pity. Some of it was good, as I said.'

'What was it about?'

'About George Eliot. It was also an attack on some of those newer literary theories in quite unguarded terms. Indeed, it was more about the theorists than the theories, and attributed some unlikely practices to them.'

'Could your client not have excised those portions and got it published?'

'That's my point. A normal person would have paid attention to what a publisher said—it's a publisher's business to know these things. He would also have taken the advice of their lawyers—and mine too once I had seen the problem. But no. Emery's view was that he having written his book, it would be a betrayal of his integrity were it not to be published exactly as he had written it. And for him to acquiesce in revision . . . you can imagine his reaction to the suggestion that he should, as it were, help to mutilate his work by doing the cutting himself. Nor would he let anyone else tamper with it.'

'I'm beginning to think I can see how he would react.'

'There was one later book I had to help him disentangle himself from. He had signed a contract which allowed the publisher to edit the book as he considered necessary. When the proofs arrived . . .' The old man raised his hands.

Just then the secretary came in. She was young and fussed around inexpertly with the tea. Cranford watched her tolerantly, and when she had gone took up the conversation as if there had been no gap.

'That took some getting out of. He was all for suing the publisher, but then he allowed me to see the contract. I insisted that before raising the action against the publisher I had to see the contract he had entered into. And there it was—the right to edit, unfettered. Eventually it was settled, but Emery had to pay for the costs that the publisher had incurred. That was not cheap. Not cheap. But Emery had "preserved his integrity", as he put it.' The old man's tone indicated his view.

'I understand that Emery was divorced.'

'Yes. A peculiar business, that.' Cranford fell silent, turning his head to the window. Outside a blackbird perched on a branch close to the window began to sing. Cranford sighed, and turned back to Mason.

'I've never been sure whether I did right then,' he said.

Mason tilted his head.

'You're down from Scotland, aren't you?'

'Yes.'

'Done any Law—apart from the police stuff?'

'Yes. I did a Law degree as part of my training.'

'Did you, indeed.' Cranford looked at Mason keenly. 'That's a good idea. Perhaps you will understand, then.' He paused, sorting out his thoughts.

'It must have been about a quarter of a century ago. At any rate it was before the Divorce Reform Act of—was it 1969?'

Mason shrugged. He did not know.

'No matter. It was before we got into this appalling "breakdown of marriage" muddle—makes divorce too easy and devalues marriage itself, I think. No matter. Before that, getting a divorce here in England was difficult. I knew that things were more than bad between Emery and his wife. Her health was suffering, and life was bad for the child as well.' He nodded to himself. 'Yes. It was bad.'

Mason waited.

'She was from somewhere near Edinburgh, so one time when she left him—it happened occasionally when things got too bad—I got in touch with a friend of mine up there. The upshot was that she got a divorce up there on grounds of mental cruelty.'

'But the Scottish courts wouldn't have had jurisdiction,' Mason said, sitting bolt upright.

'Technically, no,' said the old man. 'But you forget that I was Emery's lawyer. The case was undefended. We used an accommodation address for serving the writs. It was better all round. Good for her, good for the child, and good for Emery himself.'

Mason shook his head briskly as if to clear it.

'Now, young man. Just sit a minute and think,' said Cranford quietly.

Mason thought.

'Was there anything about that in the letters?' asked Cranford.

'Yes. He was very bitter. Reading that material, it looked to me as if the shock of the divorce blighted his life, and set him off on a track where he gathered enemies.'

'I wondered about that, but I can assure you that he was a bitter man long before the divorce. My thought is that the shock in fact did good, for it liberated him from what was really a most unsuitable marriage. He was a natural bachelor. She hadn't the strength to stand properly against him. Indeed, I have sometimes thought that she was spared being hanged because of what Alistair and I did.'

'Alistair?'

'My friend in Edinburgh.'

'Hanged?'

'I think,' Cranford spoke very calmly, 'that Marion Emery was close to the end of her tether when we managed to free her, and that if that had not happened she would have poisoned him. She hadn't the strength to kill him otherwise—not in a direct attack, and she wouldn't have had the nerve to use a breadknife when he was asleep. No. She would have used poison, but clumsily. She would have been hanged.' He shook his head.

'But hanging went out in 1965. Come to that, I'm not sure it was available for poisoning for some time before that.'

Cranford ignored the problem. 'Was it, then? Perhaps my

memory is not as good as it might have been. But in any event she would have spent long years in prison. A poisoner cannot trade on sympathy. If she had split his head with a spade, a good plea in mitigation could have been made— but not if she accomplished the same end by stealth.'

'So you persuaded Emery not to make a fuss?'

'Exactly. It was the best all round.'

'And he accepted that?'

'He accepted that if he did defend the action all sorts of allegations might be made about him.'

'But that doesn't square with his attitude to publishing,' objected Mason.

Just then the intercom buzzed. Cranford spoke briefly to his secretary. He would see a client next day at 9.30.

'I see your point,' he resumed. 'But you will just have to accept that, like most people, my client was not completely consistent in his behaviour, or sometimes his attitudes. He was badly hurt. I convinced him that he would be more hurt if he fought.'

'Though he was your client?'

'You mean that it was my part only to do as he instructed me?'

Mason nodded.

'I have already given you the answer to that. The health and well-being of the wife and the child was at stake. Divorce was better in this instance. One promises "till death" and in this case the marriage was dead.'

'That's not the interpretation I would put on the phrase, but I see what you mean, and in any case it is all far in the past.'

'Now perhaps you could give me some information.'

Mason looked up, surprised.

'Your presence indicates to me that there is some mystery about my client's death. As his Executor I have a right to know, especially as it may alter the disposal of the estate.'

'Will it?'

Cranford opened a drawer in his desk and slid a large folded sheet of paper across to Mason. 'You had better read this,' he said.

'This' proved to be Emery's will. It briefly provided that all Emery's estate was to go to his daughter unless she were 'involved' in his death. In that case Cranford as Executor was to 'pay, convey and make over the whole of my estate (after paying all my debts and funeral expenses) to the Chancellor of the Exchequer for the time being for the mitigation (so far as my poor contribution may) of the National Debt. The Chancellor has had so much of my worldly goods that he may as well have the rest.'

'He seems to have had a sense of humour,' observed Mason as he handed it back.

'A curious, spasmodic sense of humour, but when on form he could be very funny. Would you like a copy?'

'Please. Though I do not think that you will be called on to comply with the conditional bequest.'

'I hope not. But as you are here I presume that your inquiries are not yet at an end.'

'No.'

The two men sat silent for a moment, and then Mason put his thought into words.

'Did you know the nature of Mr Emery's connection with the *New Inquirer*?'

The old man smiled. 'Yes.'

'Did he tell you?'

'No.'

'Then how . . .?'

'It was one of those curious accidents, I suppose. I was speaking to my former secretary but one. She told me. I had been reading the Raven as long as he had been published but had not made the connection myself. But when she told me I realized that there were some mannerisms which I was familiar with—turns of phrase and the like.'

'You knew him well enough to spot that?'

'Yes. In retrospect, you understand. I think I said we met at the golf club and I used to go out there even when I had given up actually golfing. It's a nice clubhouse and the people are, well, pleasant. Mostly. Perhaps Emery was an exception. But somehow I and one or two other members liked him. I think he came for the company too.'

'And the secretary? How did she know?'

'Ah yes. You may have noticed my secretary just now is a young lady.'

Mason nodded.

'I don't do much work nowadays, and so it has been agreed that it is I who deal with the new girls. Once they have learned the work of the office with my relatively leisurely pace, they move on. Sometimes they marry out, and sometimes they get jobs in another office, and sometimes if we have a vacancy elsewhere, they go to some of the other partners or assistants.

'I had one secretary, two back I think it was. Frankly she wasn't very good, and we were glad when she left us to get married. It spared us the awkwardness of . . .' He waved his hand in the air.

Mason smiled. He knew the problem.

'She was a bit neurotic. But I met her in the street a year or so ago, with her pram, out shopping. She said she was typing for Walter Emery quite regularly, as well as doing theses for students and those sort of things. And she asked if I knew that he wrote as the Raven. She had seen something in the *Inquirer* that she had previously typed. Of course, I told her that she ought not to tell anyone what she had said to me—I knew how he might react, for example, and it *was* a private matter. But it was interesting to know. It added to the interest of his reviews and comments.' He laughed wheezily once more.

'And now, perhaps, you have something to tell me?' he asked. 'Why are you here? How did Emery die?'

'Before I answer those questions, might I ask another?'

'Surely.'

'Are you in touch with Emery's widow or daughter? Can you give me addresses?'

'Yes.' The old man produced a looseleaf alphabetical address book and gave Mason a note of the address of both mother and daughter. It was in Manchester, New Hampshire, USA. 'She wanted to get away, and as a highly trained medical secretary, she had no trouble emigrating. She had a brother over there as well.'

'Have they ever been back?'

'The odd trip, perhaps, but I'm not sure about that.'

'Have you seen either of them recently?'

'No. I remember seeing the daughter when she was ten or so, a lovely child with dark hair and a fair complexion. She was over with her mother. I think her name was Lucy, but I haven't seen them for years.'

'Have you been in touch with either?'

'In the circumstances I have deferred getting in touch with them, except to write a short note of condolence.'

'So the girl knows nothing about her inheritance?'

'Not unless her father told her—but I think that he would not have done so.'

Mason sighed and nodded. 'Emery died of heart failure, which may have been brought on by a physical attack—there was a bruise on his face—or perhaps was brought on by an altercation. Or it might be that he was heading for heart problems in any case and his bath was just too warm following that sort of upset. That's as far as I would want to go at present. But there is evidence that there was an argument in his room the evening that he died.'

'But no one did anything about it?'

'One couple were going to complain. But they didn't. He

was found by the maid next morning, in the bath. The manager knew that there was a doctor having his breakfast and went and called him. He was a colleague of mine, on the last morning of his holiday.' Mason spread his hands, raising his left eyebrow. Cranford smiled too at the irony of it.

'But there is something else that you are not telling me.' Cranford made the words a statement not a question.

Mason shrugged. 'I would be grateful if you would keep our conversation entirely confidential for the present,' he said, rising to his feet.

'Surely,' replied Cranford, also rising.

'Now,' said Mason. 'I had better not take up more of your time. But perhaps you could also give me an address for the former secretary you mentioned?'

'Oh dear,' said Cranford. 'I hope I have not got her into trouble.'

'Not at all. It's just that I am trying to get a picture of the deceased clear in my mind, and if I can talk to as many as possible who knew him, it helps. If she was working for him, she may have seen some side to him that was hidden from others.'

'It seems a great deal to undertake all this work if you are uncertain as to how he died. It sounds more to me as if you are pursuing a murder inquiry.' Cranford glanced sidelong at Mason as he again thumbed his way through the address book.

Mason smiled.

'Here we are. Mrs Monica Farrell.' He held the book out to Mason.

2

Monica Farrell was small, untidy, pregnant and over-stressed.

'Could I talk to you about something important?' asked

Mason after he had identified himself at her door.

She glanced over her shoulder and, as if on cue, a child started wailing somewhere inside.

'Come in,' she said and bolted back indoors. 'You'll just need to put up with it all if it's important.'

Mason found her in a small kitchen cradling a child which had just bumped his head. She kissed it better, opened the back door and encouraged him to leave.

'Now?' she said, dumping herself on a kitchen chair.

Mason looked around, but the other chair had a pile of washing on it.

'Oh dear,' she said. 'Come through here.'

The room she led the way into was not much better. An ironing board was set up in front of the fireplace, and clothes were piled on a sofa just to one side. She fussed a bit, clearing somewhere for him to sit, and sat down across the room.

'I'm making some inquiries into a death. Someone I gather you know. The late Mr Walter Emery.'

'Eh?' Her hands went to her face. 'Him? Dead?'

'You hadn't heard? It was in some of the papers.'

'No time to read any papers round here. Tom's nineteen months and whatever's due in a couple of weeks. No time to do anything but housework.'

'Well, I'm sorry to have to tell you that Mr Emery died a week last Saturday. It was a sudden death, so we are having to make some inquiries—which is why I'm here. It won't take long.'

'I see.'

'I understood that you occasionally typed for him.'

'Yes.'

'What kind of a person was he?'

She shook her head. 'Him. Dead! I can't believe it.'

'It happened up in Scotland.'

She went still, and looked warily up at Mason.

'He was found dead in his bath. At his hotel.'

She whitened and turned her head away. 'What have I to do with that? I had nothing to do with it.' She spoke quickly.

'It's just that I was down here in connection with the death and gathered that you had worked for him. Did you know where he had gone on holiday?'

'Who told you I typed for him?' Her lips were pinched together and she had begun to breathe jerkily.

'That doesn't matter. You knew where he had gone?'

'He always went there.'

'Yes. I believe he did.' Mason nodded, pleasantly. 'What was he like to work for?'

She relaxed visibly and looked at Mason, her colour returning. Mason found himself remembering the breathing exercises his wife Jane had practised prior to the birth of their son. 'I didn't do all that much for him. He was fussy. A nuisance,' said Monica Farrell.

'A nuisance?'

She shrugged. 'He never liked corrections. Really fussy. I had to retype a page if there was as much as one correction in it.'

'And did he change his text once you had typed it?'

She nodded. 'That too. Sometimes he'd get a page redone several times. I've seen him come round quite late at night about something or other. Piffling really. Never seemed to care. Upsetting the youngster's sleep with the bell. And would he keep his voice down?'

'You mean he was inconsiderate?'

She nodded again.

'Did he pay well?'

'Not very. Not for the sort of service he wanted.'

'Did you tell him so?'

'You couldn't tell him nothing.'

'He sounds unpleasant. Why did you carry on working for him?'

She shrugged her shoulders again. 'He was difficult to speak to—to refuse.' She smiled secretively. 'But I got . . .' She stopped, her lips pinched together once more.

Quickly Mason bridged the chasm that seemed about to develop. 'What sort of thing did he write?'

'You know about that I should think. If you're any good.'

It was Mason's turn to nod.

'Would you happen to have any of his work here? A carbon or something?' he asked.

'Yes. Probably. Just a minute. He left something to be ready for when he came back.' She got up and went out of the room.

She came back bearing several sheets. 'He left this to be done. I was expecting him to collect it this week.'

'Can I have a look?'

'Sure. There's no one else'll be interested now, I expect. Unless . . .' She stopped.

Mason looked at the typescript and smiled. It was a book review in the familiar style. The lead paragraph read:

This book is priced at £18.95. Were it to contain a £20 note pinned inside its cover, it might be thought to be worth purchasing. Other than a note of a higher denomination, there are no other circumstances to commend it.

'I see you use a proportional spacing typehead on a standard electric machine,' Mason said quietly, taking from his inside pocket the letter which Clarence Berman had received. He unfolded it and held it up beside the book review. He was looking from the one to the other when there was a gasp from Monica Farrell. She had gone parchment white and was grasping her belly.

3

While Mason was phoning for an ambulance and summoning Monica Farrell's husband from his work, Ian Crawford finished his lunch and set off up the Knoll.

He was getting thoroughly tired of this case. Despite all that had happened, it still seemed to him that the best explanation was that Emery had died of natural causes. Oh, he had been disliked—justifiably. But neither that nor the anonymous Berman letter converted his death into a murder. Still, the case had the advantage of Lucrezia Gottman—he wished idly as he climbed that they had met in other circumstances, then grinned as he caught himself. He was sure that she had nothing to do with it. Perhaps later, when it was all over . . .?

He found her sitting as before, tucked into the grassy spot sheltered by the birches, a large notepad on her lap.

'How's the bite?' she asked as he spread his jacket and sat down beside her.

'Not bad,' he said, rolling up his sleeve. She looked at the red lump with its yellowed top where pus was gathering.

'Doesn't look all right to me,' she said. 'I think you should take that to the doctor.'

'No. It's nothing,' he said, buttoning his cuff.

'I mean it. These things can be quite nasty if they're left.'

'It'll be all right in a few days.'

'Have you been bitten like that before?'

'Um. No.'

'Well, there you are. That looks like quite a reaction to me. You would be better with some proper anti-histamine ointment. I should have given you the tube to use over the weekend. Maybe that would have been best.'

He shrugged. 'Chopping off more heads, are you?' he asked, pointing at the pad.

She smiled and turned over the top three or four pages.
'It's going quite well, I think.' Then she laughed. 'I think
I shocked your superior.'

Crawford grinned. 'Maybe not him, but you certainly
shocked me. How come a head like yours can come out with
something like that?'

'Market forces.'

'Explain.'

She became solemn. 'It's quite simple, really. The more
copies a book sells the more money it makes. Right?'

He nodded.

'My novel sold just less than three hundred copies.'

'Thanks to that review?'

She shook her head, sending the black hair swirling round
her shoulders. 'Despite the review. Or maybe even because
of it. They say that any review is better than silence.'

Crawford looked surprised, but she did not notice.

'Your first problem is getting published at all, but after
that the main problem is getting sales. Do you know how
many titles were published in the UK last year?'

He shook his head.

'Over ninety thousand.'

'Ah.'

'How many titles does your average bookshop stock?'

He paused, then spoke slowly. 'But isn't there something
about writing that makes you write? I thought that was the
reason most people did it.'

'My novel was like that. I would like to write more of
what suits me, but I'm tired of being poor and having to
take orders from men, most of whom I don't respect. I'm
tired of little stories about a pigeon-fancying parking warden
who's just won a cup at the local show, or a hospital row,
and all the hundred and one bits of trivia that go into the
modern local newspaper.'

'But you know there are other forms of journalism.'

'I can't find the way in to that. You've got to be lucky as well as good, and I'm not.'

'Your uncle . . .'

She looked at him, scorn in her voice. 'I wouldn't ask for help.'

'So?'

'So I want to write something that'll sell. I've read and analysed what seems to sell just now, and I think I can deliver it. This—' she tapped the sheets of paper—'is it.'

He nodded, uncertain how to proceed.

At length he asked, 'Was that review by the Raven very bad?'

She tossed her head. 'It wasn't good.'

'But it hurt deeply.' Crawford spoke quietly. 'Any special reason?'

She looked out over the valley where birds were wheeling in the air before speaking. 'What got me was that he knew me and used what he knew in demolishing me.'

'I don't understand.' Still quietly.

She turned angrily to look at him. 'I was a student of his down at Wessex. He remembered me.'

Crawford stilled himself and frowned, looking interested but puzzled. 'Are you sure about that? I thought you said he didn't remember people?'

'I am sure he remembered the name, and saw things in the book that he could tie in with me. That's what made that review so bloody wounding. Oh, the book had flaws— I know that. But to have personal things brought in . . . so damn skilfully too. I couldn't sue.'

'So that's how you quarrelled with him?'

She laughed without humour, sitting ramrod straight. 'It was funny. I met him in the main drive and introduced myself. He had forgotten my face—like I said, he was never any good with faces. But when I told him exactly who I was and exactly what I thought of him . . .' She looked off into the distance, and humour came with a giggle. 'I called him a cowardly, lying, inadequate human being and I was glad that at least his colleagues had seen through him, because that doubtless explained why he was still a lecturer.'

'I bet that hurt.'

'I also said I could quite understand why his wife had left him. No woman would put up with a slug like him.'

'You knew about his marriage?'

'Yes. It was part of student knowledge at Wessex.'

'So I gather you're quite pleased he's dead?'

She slumped her shoulders and pulled at some grass. 'No,' she said at last, thoughtfully, not looking at Crawford. 'No. Oh, I remember what I said to you and your boss, but no. I didn't mean all that. There's good in everyone. Everyone dies with some of it undone. I grieve for unfulfilledness in anyone.'

'Did you ever visit him here. In his room? A week last Friday?'

'Certainly not!'

'Did you see him apart from that time on the drive?'

'What is this? Are you on duty?'

'So you wouldn't in fact have cut off his head and his hands?'

She shuddered with distaste. 'Oh no. It's one thing to write about it, but the thought of actually . . .' She threw the grass away.

'Did you know he was here before you came?'

She looked at him from under her fringe.

'Did you?' he persisted. 'You did know!' He spoke, taking knowledge from her eyes.

'Well, actually . . .'

'Was it an anonymous letter?'

She was suddenly silent. He could see her running their conversation through her mind.

'Typed.'

'Yes.' A very small voice.
'Do you still have it?'
'Yes.'
'Here?'
'In my room.'
He got to his feet. 'Shall wc go?'

4

At the Department of English of Wessex University that afternoon Mason received a formal, distant welcome. Had it not been summer, Mason would have said that it was frosty. He was getting nowhere, fast. It was not that he was being stone-walled. There just seemed to be nothing to find out.

'I really do not see how we can be of assistance to you,' said the spindly Professor of English eventually. 'Naturally I regret the death of a colleague, and the circumstances you describe are unfortunate, but . . .' He shrugged.

'Perhaps his death will help you meet your target for staffing levels?' hazarded Mason in an attempt to get behind the façade.

The corners of the Professor's mouth dipped. 'That remark is in very poor taste.'

'I'm sorry. It's just I saw in the paper this morning that you too are having cuts. Just like my local university back home. It's a miserable business, and quite demanding on persons in authority.'

The Professor frowned. 'There is no doubt that Emery's death will have an effect in that regard.'

'Will he be missed?'

'I doubt it.'

'You say he was a lecturer. I wonder why he was still only a lecturer. That must be unusual for someone of his age. Not to have had promotion, I mean.'

'There were reasons. He wrote little. I tried to encourage him when I first came here, but he rebuffed me. After that we had little communication other than what was necessary. Occasionally I had to draw to his attention complaints from the students—he could be terribly rude to students.'

'But nothing that would have led to his dismissal.'

'No.' The word was brief. Suddenly, from the glitter in the Professor's eye as he replied, Mason got the momentary impression that the Professor would have seized an opportunity to have got rid of Emery. But clearly Mason was wasting his own time, and the Professor felt he was wasting his. He decided to cut his losses.

'I see,' said Mason, getting to his feet. 'Is there anyone else that he was close to that I should have a word with?'

'I suppose there's Dr Caspar.'

Dr Caspar was a man of roughly Emery's age.

'No. I don't suppose that people will really miss Emery. We were shocked of course to hear of his death—in the midst of life, etcetera—but it's different when it happens to someone you know.' He shook his head.

'He was never promoted above the lecturer range?'

Caspar shook his head. 'Little written in an area where there is an over-supply of academics with books. And also there was his fine talent for getting on the wrong side of people.'

Mason lifted his broken eyebrow. Caspar explained.

'I'd say his last chance of promotion came just after there was a change of Vice-Chancellors here. He'd been rude to the previous one, but to Willoughby . . .' Caspar shook his head wonderingly. 'I was there. The new man had been through the usual list of inviting Heads of Department and the like and then one evening he invited some of the older lecturers and senior lecturers. Emery had had a bit much to drink, I suppose, though it never really showed with him.

He sat on Willoughby's sofa in his own house and told him that the Vice-Chancellor and the Administration had the same function in a University as the janitors. They were there to look after buildings. Their sole justification was merely to provide the likes of him with heat, light, shelter, books and secretarial facilities.'

Mason laughed. 'Janitors?'

'Yes.'

'So that was that?'

'Well, of course it was. As I said, Emery hadn't written any books. Anyone who's worth his salt—and a lot of who aren't—have written at least one and often more than one. Books are . . . are . . .' he groped for a word . . . 'common. So, in the Corleone phrase, he couldn't make either the Department or Willoughby an offer they couldn't refuse.'

'Did he try? I mean, are there unpublished MSS in his desk drawer?'

'I don't know. But somehow I don't think so. Most people don't say what they're working on in case it doesn't get a publisher. Such things are confidential. But he never said anything that I can recall that would have shown he had something on the stocks. He did make the odd remark you could construe as oblique disappointment in publishers, but . . .'

'Such as?'

'Hmm. I remember one comment on a colleague's book: "Never mind the quality, feel the weight."' Caspar smiled as he spoke.

'Would you say Emery was a bitter man?'

'Yes. Of course he was. He saw people who he thought no good get on better than him. Some of them he had taught.'

'Which would add to the offence?'

'Naturally.'

'Did the bitterness show other than in those oblique comments?'

'Well, he really had little time for his colleagues. Latterly he even gave up coming for coffee.'

'What about meetings?'

'He came to those. Sometimes made good points.'

'His teaching—did it suffer?'

'No. I don't think it did. He made it clear to the students that he thought they were freeloaders, comfortable on government grants, and that he held them in complete contempt. But a very few of the very good ones responded to his attitude. In a perverse sort of way he liked it like that. Sometimes he got an answering spark. And there were one or two that he in an odd sort of way . . . triggered. They took fire through anger, and the intellectual wrestling between them brought them on no end.'

'You know that? Or did you just hear about it?'

'Sometimes he invited me to a seminar he ran for senior students. And sometimes he would say something about this one or that outside of class. You could tell. I think myself that—' Caspar leaned close to Mason—'that he loved some of the folk he taught, but was desperate in case they would see it. Some sort of substitute for family.' Caspar leaned back.

'Could be,' replied Mason. 'But you two got on all right?'

'Most of the time, yes. We had a common affection for Ambrose Bierce.'

'Ah!'

'Look him up, man. You'll have a treat.'

'Didn't Bierce write a story about a son shooting his father in the Civil War?

'An educated policeman! I must make a note in my diary.'

'So Bierce helped?'

'Yes. We would quote from *The Devil's Dictionary*. That usually bridged a disagreement. If we fell out, we would fall back in after a day or so using "Brother Ambrose", as we used to call him.'

'Did he fall out with his students and fall back in again?'

'Yes.'

'So how were things reconciled between him and a student?'

'Now that was different. When he fell out with someone he would ignore him. The "restoration" was by him starting to address the student again. Usually he would suddenly growl something wholly sarcastic about the student, but that meant that the target had been restored to favour. It wasn't a wholly satisfactory way to run things. Some realized what was going on, but they still didn't like him.'

'Did students ever complain?'

'Sometimes. Someone would go to the Professor and he would say something to Emery, but that didn't help a bit. Reconciliation just took time, each time.'

'But there was always some sort of tacit reconciliation?'

'It was more that Emery indicated a truce rather than reconciliation. And much depended on whether the truce happened close to the end of the session. I'm sure some went away from here angry about his treatment of them, and most hated his guts while they were here. But I've met others from years ago who in retrospect respect what he did for them with his way of going about things.'

'Did they ever say so to him?'

'I couldn't say.'

'Did he ever not "declare a truce", as you put it?'

'Hmmm. Once. A few years back. He caught a student plagiarizing in a piece of assessed work that was to count in the final result. He was death on unattributed quotation in essays if he spotted it.'

'So what happened?'

'The fellow left. He was foolish. He had got the bulk of his work from two sources—arcane sources, to be sure. I think there was an odd form of words which Emery recognized, so he hunted, and eventually annotated the dissertation. Book X, page Y, line Z, and so on opposite most of the paragraphs. An open and shut case. The fellow had a temper and just up and left when he was accused. Walter was a bit distressed, I remember, for in his eyes the fellow had promise. But it was a fair cop, as you might say.' Caspar smiled coyly at his own joke. 'He wouldn't wait to be dealt with. He just up and left. Wounded pride at being found out, I suppose. Maybe not. He didn't like Walter, and Walter had him dead to rights—no way out.'

'Couldn't he have argued the penalty? A plea in mitigation, as I would call it?'

'He had absolutely no basis to argue from. But you're right, he could have salvaged things by a plea for mercy— got a reprimand, and a reduced mark for the work, I suppose.'

'Emery must have had a remarkable memory to be able to spot something like that.'

'Yes. But Walter could do that. He had a very retentive memory. Good memory—just not very good at sorting things out with it.'

'Did he bear a grudge long—given that memory?'

Caspar nodded slowly. 'I'm afraid so. Occasionally he would make a comment about something that happened in the Department, say, years and years ago. That showed that he brooded over things, slights and so on.'

'Was he a good hater?'

Caspar gave a slight, humourless laugh. 'Yes.'

'Would anyone here have hated him? In return, as it were.'

Caspar paused. 'No. I don't think so,' he replied at last. 'Not on staff. He was a sort of natural phenomenon you just accepted, like the weather. You tried not to get soaked by a downpour, but if it happened, well . . . he would go away and life would be all right again.'

'Was he a sort of University character?'

'No. He wasn't that visible round the University. Other than his students, no one saw him all that regularly. I suppose I'm the one who saw most of him, and that wasn't much.'

'Had he hobbies?'

'I don't know. I think he took to golf at one time, but I don't know if he persisted with it. I wouldn't expect so.'

'What about his family?'

Caspar looked up at the ceiling. 'You've heard about that, have you?'

'A little.'

'It was better that they split up. Really, he was one of those men that should never have married.'

'Did the break-up affect him?'

There was a pause while Caspar considered. 'Yes. He was arrogant before, but it gave an iciness to it.'

'Was his arrogance well based?'

'I don't know what you mean by that.'

'Was he so good that he excelled others to the extent that any arrogance might be justified?'

Again Caspar paused, marshalling his thoughts. 'He didn't excel. He was precise. Intolerant of other viewpoints. The rudeness was a shield for his own inadequacies.'

'But you said he was a good teacher.'

'I didn't. I said that his attitude occasionally triggered good people. He inspired them to excel so as to stand up to his assaults. That's not being a good teacher. It's a technique which works with a few good folk. It brings them on— makes them stand on their own feet. But for the average student—and most students are average—he was a disaster. He crushed them.'

'So he was hated by the students?'

'Undoubtedly.'

5

Lucrezia Gottman's letter looked as though it was exactly the same as the one Clarence Berman had received.

'I'll need to keep this,' Crawford said.

She nodded.

'And we'll need to talk to you again. Probably tomorrow.'

Again she nodded.

Back in the room which had been set aside for police use Crawford found Paget talking to a middle-aged man.

'Here's who we need,' said Paget. 'Mr Crawford, sir. This is Mr . . . Mr . . .'

'Armstrong,' said the other, holding out his hand.

'And what can I do for you?' asked Crawford once the formalities were over.

'I was down at the Monzie office,' said Paget, 'and Brian Phelps down there told me that they had just had a phone call from Mr Armstrong about an anonymous letter.'

Crawford put his hand to his inside pocket. Three anonymous letters? They were falling like leaves.

Paget did not notice the movement, and carried on. 'It seemed to me that there might be some connection with the illnesses that were reported, so I waited for him to come in and brought him up.' He waved a hand at Armstrong, inviting him to take over.

Armstrong produced an envelope from his pocket.

'I thought I should bring this to the police,' he said, opening it and giving Crawford a sheet of paper. Pasted on it in letters clearly clipped from a newspaper was the message:

u H T MILK is offAL

Crawford looked at Armstrong. 'Where did you get this?' he asked.

'I'm the manager of the local dairy. It was slipped under the door sometime last night. At least it was there when we opened up this morning.'

'And you waited until the afternoon to take it to the police?'

Armstrong reddened. 'We are very busy. It didn't seem to me to be terribly important.'

Crawford stared at him.

Armstrong began to stammer. 'That's right. Of course. My father-in-law said there had been people sick here. Perhaps there's a connection. That would be awful.'

'Your father-in-law?'

'Dan Sassella. He's the night porter—or one of them.'

'Ah.' Crawford laid the sheet of paper down on his desk. 'I understand,' he said. 'Thank you for your cooperation and helpfulness. I wonder if—to keep things right—you would give Inspector Paget here a short statement about how this message came into your possession.'

'Yes, I can do that,' said Armstrong, though the sidelong look he gave Crawford indicated that on another occasion he would think twice about trying to be helpful.

Seeing it, Crawford cursed himself for his stiltedness. How would Mason have put the matter? Doubtless there would have been a soothing stream of 'just routine' or 'it's terrible the amount of paper we have to use, but regulations require us to . . .' Anything to calm the man. He could hear Mason's voice in memory: 'They have to *know* they are helping us, even if they aren't, and that *we* wouldn't ourselves dream of putting them to this trouble but we're compelled to go through the routine. You say that sort of thing even if we aren't. If they're at ease, more will come. The most milk comes from contented cows.'

'Do many people object to UHT milk round here?' he asked Armstrong.

'Well, it hasn't really taken on. It's mostly the hotels and guest-houses that use UHT. It helps them. The portions are individually measured out so there's not much waste, and folk don't go wild the way they can with a milk-jug. It's more economical for the hotels. That's its main advantage as well as it keeping for so long. But most of our ordinary customers still get their milk delivered every day.' His stammer had almost gone as he spoke about familiar matters.

'Didn't the EEC have some scheme to require us to give up deliveries?'

'That's right, but nothing will come of that.' Armstrong was most definite.

'Was there any opposition to UHT milk when it started?'

Armstrong reflected. 'I see the point of your asking.' He considered. 'Now that you mention it, there was some opposition at one point. When people thought that they would be forced to use UHT and that ordinary milk would be stopped there was quite a lot in the papers and some letters to the dairy. But all that died down some time ago.'

'No one was ultra—um—vehement?'

'Not unduly. There were a couple of letters in very strong terms, but nothing untoward. I rather sympathized.' Armstrong laughed. 'I hate the taste of UHT myself.'

'And no one tampered with any of it?'

Armstrong shook his head. 'I hope there's no question of that,' he said, 'but in any event that wouldn't be our fault. Our products are well sterilized.'

'Do you produce UHT milk?'

Armstrong stared at him. 'Of course,' he said. 'How silly of me. No. We merely distribute. We bottle our local milk, but we only distribute the UHT.' He seemed relieved by the realization that if there was something wrong it had happened elsewhere.

'Oh well, If you could just give the Inspector your statement about how the letter was found, and anything else you remember, we'll pass it on. You can do that here,' he added to Paget.

6

Dr Lloyd's surgery was needing a coat of paint, and the man himself looked as though he still needed a holiday.

He was apologetic. 'Yes, the police were in touch, but I thought it was just a routine inquiry and asked the locum to deal with it. Then they asked again.'

'That must have been some days ago,' replied Mason drily.

'I did give them a letter. Friday, I think.' Dr Lloyd opened the file. 'Yes. Here you are.' He passed the file over.

The letter was terse. Emery had shown some symptoms of raised blood pressure when he had last consulted the doctor—about two years before. He had not been back since.

'So you have no recent knowledge of his condition?'

'None, I'm afraid.' He saw Mason's question form before it was spoken. 'We're too hard pressed here to chase up our patients. We've got enough to do to cope with the ones that come to us—or call us in.'

'But you aren't surprised to hear that he has died, probably from a heart attack?'

Lloyd shrugged. 'No. He was the type. Under-exercised. What they used to call "choleric".' He pursed his lips. 'No. I'd not have quoted odds on a coronary for him.'

'Was he under any medication?'

Lloyd shook his head and tapped the file. 'Not that I

know of. He had acute catarrh, but you can't do anything for that.'

'He wouldn't have been treating himself?'

Lloyd hesitated. 'I'm not sure what you mean by that.'

Mason regrouped his thought. 'Was he the kind of person who would have tried to treat himself "over the counter" as it were, or through a homeopath?'

'I doubt it.'

'What sort of things did he consult you about—in the past?'

'Just the usual minor ailments. 'Flu and assorted viruses. The occasional sore throat—he was a lecturer, as you know. There was the catarrh I mentioned. I believe he was operated on for that when he was younger, before he came to us. It was a fashionable operation at one time—sort of washing the sinuses—but as happened in a good many cases, it failed. Left him with an impaired sense of taste too. Taste is mostly smell, you know.'

Mason nodded. He had an aunt who had suffered in that way. 'You said he was under-exercised. Did you know he was a member of a golf club?' he asked.

'Was he? That does surprise me. But then was he a player or was it the convenience of the clubhouse?' Lloyd smiled deprecatingly.

'He wouldn't have had any contact with phenelzine sulphate?'

'Certainly not. Nor with any of those trypsin inhibitors. I would have considered that sort of treatment very risky for someone of his age and build. Why do you ask?' Lloyd's eyes had narrowed.

Mason shrugged. 'Just a thought,' he said.

'No. We are very careful what we give patients with a predisposition to heart or blood pressure trouble.'

'He had a predisposition, then?'

'I speak loosely, and from recollection. As I said, he hasn't been to see us for a couple of years. But he was the type. Certainly he would have been checked for pressure before we put him on anything that would have affected that end of things. But we haven't seen him. As far as we are concerned he was a normal patient. Better than normal. I would say that latterly he troubled us less than many others.'

'Nothing odd in his history at all?'

Lloyd riffled through the notes, and closed the file again.

'Not really. I had him on a tranquillizer after his divorce, but that wasn't needed for very long.'

'I see.' Mason got to his feet. 'Do you think I might take this file for a few days? I'll let you have it back.'

'It is irregular, but . . . well, all right.'

Mason was almost out of the door when he turned. 'Oh, there is one other thing I meant to ask.'

Lloyd looked up inquiringly.

'Emery was using a French dental fixative. Would you know why?'

Lloyd laughed. 'Still?' he asked.

'Why do you ask?' Mason's surprise at the question showed.

'It's some years back. Emery had had an embarrassment once when he had trouble with his teeth in front of a class. He went on holiday in France and came back with some brand or other that he thought was the best thing for teeth since rivets. But he wanted it on the National Health. His dentist refused to put forward a case, so he came to me.'

'And?'

'We failed.'

'But you did try?'

'Yes. At least I wrote a letter, I remember, but they turned it down. They said if I would certify that Emery needed it basically as a matter of mental health, they would reconsider.'

'And did you?'

'No. Emery wasn't one to concede in any way that perhaps his mental condition wasn't all it might be.'

'And was it?'

Lloyd shrugged. 'Takes all sorts,' he said.

'The reasons for some are obscure,' replied Mason.

7

Lucrezia Gottman was glad she had a date that evening. The afternoon had been uncomfortable. Crawford's swift change from being a pleasant companion to a chilled detachment had been very disturbing. Oh, she had been foolish not to have told him and his boss—what was his name again?—Mason. She should have told them all that she knew of Walter Emery as soon as they had said what they were about. Now, clearly, she had got herself into a corner. Why had she assumed that she alone had received that letter? The Raven was well-known for savage reviews. Why had she thought that she alone had got that information?

But it was too late now. She would just have to live with the consequences. No point in worrying about it. There were other pressing matters for the immediate future. She tossed her head, and caught sight of her bedside clock. She was late. She threw a jacket over her shoulders, picked up her handbag and headed for the door. On her way out she caught sight of herself in the mirror, and pocketed a small brush in passing.

Her escort was waiting at the wheel of his yellow Triumph. The hood was down. He was drumming his fingers on the wheel. Involuntarily she tightened her jaw as she walked across the gravel. She hoped that she would not betray herself. Sometimes talking of the old days lulled one into a lack of watchfulness.

'You're late,' he said. 'I was going to give you another ninety seconds.'

She laughed as she settled herself into the comfort of the passenger seat. 'What's the hurry?'

He frowned, his knuckles whitening on the wheel. 'I said seven forty-five. I meant seven forty-five.'

It crossed her mind to ask why in that case he had waited, but she did not want to risk his temper. It was swift, but severe while it lasted.

'It's just as well I didn't wait to do my hair. I'll do it as we go.' She put the brush into the glove compartment. 'Where are we going?' she asked as they swept out of the car park.

'Greyhavens. Somewhere where I often go. Wait and see.'

They parked in the Church Street car park. He drove up to the deserted second top floor.

'Why come up here?' she asked. There had been cars only on the bottom two floors.

'When we're going I'll take you up to the top,' he said. 'The view is quite spectacular once it's properly dark.'

'Are you going to put up the hood?' she asked.

'I don't think it'll rain in here,' he said, glancing about.

The lift was out of order, so they went down the stairs and he guided her to the nightclub in the basement of the Olympus Hotel immediately across the road.

Inside, he led her to a table in the far right-hand corner where two other couples were sitting. He waved a hand at them. 'These are Lisa and Fred, Mandy and Bert.'

Lucrezia nodded politely. 'Pleased to meet you.'

Fred ignored her. 'Roy, you're late,' he said truculently to her escort. 'You're always late.'

Grogan paid no attention. 'This is Lucy,' he said, using the familiar shortening of her name. 'She's a friend from University days.' The couples looked her over. Lucrezia was not impressed. A man in a shabby raincoat got up from a seat in the corner and came over.

'Lucy,' he said, greeting her with a hug. 'Are you up for the evening or something?'

'Uncle Harry,' she replied. 'I didn't expect to see you till next week.' She cast an eye over her uncle, which he saw, and then turned to her companions.

'This is my Uncle Harry. I'm afraid I've forgotten . . .' She paused, holding up a hand to the couples. 'But this is . . .' She turned.

'Roy Grogan.' He introduced himself.

Harry Irwin nodded politely. 'Well, I'd better be on my way. Leave you youngsters to enjoy yourselves. See you next week, Lucy.'

'Yes. Fine. As arranged?'

Irwin nodded and left.

Grogan watched him go and then pulled out a seat for Lucrezia. 'What'd you like?' he asked.

After Roy had got drinks, conversation idled for a few minutes. It seemed to Lucrezia that her presence had dampened things.

'How's business?' asked Roy of Bert.

'So-so. Things always dip just now—everyone's waiting for the new car year to start, and everyone that wants one ordered it weeks ago just to be certain.'

Roy nodded.

'You sure you don't want to change yours?' asked Bert.

'Quite sure.'

'I could get you a good deal on it.'

Roy shook his head. Bert sat back. Clearly this was a re-run conversation. He dropped the matter.

Lisa nudged Fred and indicated the empty glass in front of her. He looked round the others, got up and fetched her a refill.

'Always swift off the mark,' said Bert as Fred sat down again.

'Whaddya mean?'

If you'd waited a few minutes you could've got the next round.'

Fred's face darkened. Roy intervened.

'Where's Audrey?' he asked.

'Visiting Colin,' replied Fred with an ugly smile.

'Colin had an accident at the weekend,' said Bert.

'Seems he had an argument in a lane.' Fred still smiled.

'The news is that he'll walk with a limp, and not for some time. Someone dropped a paving slab on his legs,' stated Bert.

'I am sorry to hear that,' said Roy. 'Even Greyhavens is becoming a dangerous place,' he added, turning to Lucrezia. 'All these incomers are bringing in their bad habits.'

'Is he in hospital?' she asked.

'Of course,' said Lisa scornfully.

Lucrezia, rebuffed, put her hand up to adjust her hair. 'Where's the Ladies?' she asked.

'Over there. Through the door in the corner. Left of the entrance.' It was Mandy's first contribution to the conversation. 'I'll come with you.'

In the Ladies Lucrezia found she had left her brush in the glove-box in Grogan's car.

'I'll go and get it,' she said. 'It's not far.'

'You could use mine, if you like,' said Mandy, 'but most folk like to use their own.'

'I'll not be long,' said Lucrezia, and went out.

Across the diagonal of the room she mimed brushing her hair, and went out without waiting to see whether the others had seen her.

She crossed the road and went up the stairs in the car park.

At the fifth floor she went through the doors and turned to go along to the car. It was hidden behind another which had its boot open. As her heels clicked along the concrete two men appeared from behind the nearer car.

As she came nearer she saw that the boot of Roy's car was also open.

'What are you doing?' she asked.

'None of your concern, lady. Why don't you just walk away?' came the reply from one, getting into the passenger seat of his car.

'This is my friend's car,' she said.

'Ah well. That's all right, then,' said the other man. 'We're collecting something.' He lifted a canvas hold-all from Roy's car, slammed the boot shut, tossed the bag into the back seat of his own car and got into the driver's seat.

'I'm not at all sure it is all right,' she said.

'What's the problem?' came Roy's voice behind her. He was breathing heavily.

'No problem,' said the man, getting partially out of the car. He stood with one foot on the concrete and leaned over the roof of the car. 'We explained.' He waved a hand, got into the car, started it, and drove off.

'What's all that about?' asked Lucrezia.

'Nothing. I had arranged to bring some tennis equipment up for my friend here, and he's collected it.'

'But . . .' she began, and then changed her mind. 'I came for my hairbrush,' she said, and leaning into the sports car, opened the glove-box and retrieved it.

'So Mandy said,' he replied. 'I . . . I wasn't . . . I couldn't remember if I had left the roof open, so I came to check.' He smiled, a very young smile.

'That was good of you,' she said. 'Shall we go back?'

He pursed his lips. 'We can try.'

'What's wrong?'

'I got mixed up with a table on my way out.'

'I beg your pardon?'

'There was this stupid female who got in my way. She was blocking the passage, so I went round her, but bumped their table. It was a complete accident, but the management

wasn't too impressed. I think maybe we should go somewhere else. In any case I get the impression you don't think
my friends very stimulating.'

She gave a small laugh. 'Where else is there?'

'Come on. There's another place I know of. We can leave
the car here. It's not far.'

'Fair enough. And you promised to show me the lights.'

'Later.'

CHAPTER 10

TUESDAY–WEDNESDAY

1

'I'm not sure I'm pleased to see you,' was the greeting
Raymond Pike, editor of the *New Inquirer* gave Mason as he
waved him to a chair. 'Surely the time of the police could
be better spent than coming all the way down here? To say
nothing of the expenditure of public funds involved.' He sat
down in his own plush upholstered seat, almost a caricature
of a middle-aged journal editor of the nineteen-twenties, a
resemblance aided by a set of prints on the wall behind him
of 'flappers and their escorts'.

'You indicated to my Chief Constable that you were
anxious that the death of Walter Emery should be
thoroughly investigated,' observed Mason calmly.

'I did? Yes, I believe I did. That's right. I got a formal
reply from him. Are you here as part of the "thorough
investigations"?'

Mason nodded.

'Well, Inspector, how can I help you?'

Mason was amused at Pike's transparently false failure of memory and his own demotion, but let the matter pass with a brief smile. 'I was wondering if you could explain to me several matters: how Emery came to write for you, how you found him to work with, how he was regarded. Things like that.'

Pike swivelled his chair and looked out of the window.

'As to the first, Emery and I were at school together. You could almost say we were friends. When I came to this desk he wrote a nice letter of congratulations. I got in touch.'

'You approached him?'

'In a way. We had edited the school mag together, and it seemed to me that he might well provide a certain sharpness or bite to our review section. Things were so flabby, you know, ten-twelve years back.'

'Was it not farther than that?'

Pike considered. 'I suppose it must be. No doubt you have checked your facts.'

Mason smiled again. 'I believe that it was some seventeen years ago that he started writing for you.'

'I suppose it must have been. I've been some eighteen years here when I really think it out.'

'And about seven or eight years ago he took a regular slot for you.'

Pike looked carefully at Mason. 'You seem to have been very thorough,' he observed.

'Did Emery provide the "bite" you wanted?'

'Goodness yes. Everyone knows about the Raven's articles and reviews. Even policemen, I understand.'

'Circulation rose?'

'Yes.'

'What was the point of keeping his identity secret?'

Pike swivelled round and leaned his elbows on his desk-top. 'Two purposes. One, it provided an aura of mystery. Emery knew a great deal at both first- and second-hand.'

Mason held up his hand, stopping Pike. 'By second-hand, I take it you mean that you and others supplied gossip which Emery then wove into what he wrote?'

'In another context I might object to the word "gossip", but certainly I told Walter what was going on. In a journal working in the literature field one has to know what is happening and all my reporters and staff tell me what they hear. I passed some of that on to Walter.'

'You were the only channel of communication with him? The others did not speak to him direct?'

Pike laughed, and looked almost childish. Clearly he had delighted in the air of conspiracy. 'We communicated to our respective residences. I brought his stuff in. In fact I'm sure that some of the staff here think that I wrote it. He wrote me at my home, and I wrote to him. Occasionally the great Post Office held things up, but nothing serious. Walter was very good. Fortunately we have a stock of articles and I've never had to miss a date.'

'You mean you have some unpublished material?'

'Yes. We are running another Raven review this Saturday.'

'Might I see a copy?'

Pike phoned his secretary and made arrangements for Mason to be given a photocopy of the new Raven article.

'And you have others?'

'We have one or two generalized articles. I could get them copied too if you like.'

'Please.'

Pike arranged that.

'Did you ever speak on the phone?' asked Mason as Pike put the phone down.

'Not often. As Walter used to say, the phone is too expensive for anything other than the passing of a brief message. It's better to write.'

'You were indicating the advantages of anonymity.'

Pike leaned on the desk again. 'Ah yes. So I was. The first, as I said, is the aura of mystery. The second is that the point of the article or review is made much clearer if the reader is unaffected by knowing the identity of the writer. What is said comes to his mind without overtones of prejudice or pre-conditioning.'

'It also lets the writer be, shall we say, bolder?'

Pike waved a graceful hand in a way which might have been agreement—or might not. He said nothing in reply.

'I have read a good many of the Raven articles since the matter of his death brought him to my attention—' Mason was not going to admit having read any before—'and I found myself wondering whether the *Inquirer* or Emery had ever been sued.'

Pike sat up straight. 'My dear Superintendent,' he said in shocked tones, forgetting to demote Mason. 'Of course not.'

'You have good lawyers?'

'I will admit that on occasion we have had lawyers check what was printed in the Raven column—as we do with other of our contributors. That is a matter of elementary prudence in the world of journ—of literary journalism. But we have never been sued.'

'Despite Emery's bluntness?'

'He called a spade a spade.'

'He wrote regularly for you?'

'Latterly, once every four weeks without fail, and occasionally there were other columns in the intervening weeks.'

'He selected his own material?'

'As far as articles were concerned, yes. For the book reviews, I used to send him ones that I thought would—ah —stimulate him.'

'I see.' Mason paused, looked at Pike and decided to express his thought.

'Were you close friends at school?' he asked.

Pike looked back at him.

'I can probably ask someone else,' said Mason reflectively.

Pike continue to stare at him, and then spoke in distant tones. 'Yes. We were close friends, but I fail to see the relevance of your question.'

'I suppose you were here when Emery died?'

Pike laughed suddenly as if in relief that Mason had passed to another topic. 'Yes, I suppose I have an alibi. I haven't been north of Watford for years.'

Mason nodded. 'I would be grateful if you would prepare a statement for my files delineating how you worked with Emery—the business about the barrier of secrecy and so on. Which reminds me. Did you see any of the letters which came in for the Raven?'

'No. I saw letters which came in addressed to the Editor but which in fact dealt with his column. I sent those on to him with a carbon of any reply I had thought necessary. Letters for the Raven—and there were some most months —I used to collect together and send to him in monthly batches.'

'He never let you see any?'

'No. Once or twice on the phone he would tell me the most recent threat or suggestion—some of them were quite anatomically ingenious, you know.'

'Some were biologically unlikely,' said Mason drily.

'I see. You have seen examples?'

It was Mason's turn not to reply. Instead he said: 'So your Raven may well have been protected from personal encounter, not to put it higher, by his identity being concealed.'

'Yes. Didn't I say that that was a reason for anonymity?'

'You didn't. You said it gave mystery and also sanitized the reader so that he got the message without the distortion of knowing who had written it.'

'You put that very well.'

'Was Emery's personal safety a further reason for the anonymity?

'Perhaps.' Pike shrugged.

'It seems to me to have been the main reason, if I may say so. It looks to an outsider as if the main reason for anonymity was to allow Emery to be brutal without suffering any of the normal consequences, from a literary nuclear strike to physical attack. Anyone who knew him would have been able to mount a reciprocal attack that would have eviscerated him. It would have been easy.'

'You are very passionate, Superintendent Mason.' The tone was sweet.

'I have read some of the reviews. They seemed to me to be quite immoderate—though I confess I have not read the books concerned. That they should have been written by someone who himself had not published a book seems quite wrong.'

'Truth is often uncomfortable, especially to writers. One need not have written in order to assess.'

'Those who have written know better what lies behind even a halting attempt. Some of Emery's reviews seem to be actuated by jealousy.'

'You are very eloquent.'

'No, I'm not a literary man. But that's how the Emery material generally strikes me.'

Pike shrugged again.

'Will you be able to replace him?'

'I don't know. Wait and see.'

'Can I ask one other question?'

'Please do.'

'Why did you write and ask that Emery's death be investigated? Or that it be thoroughly investigated? How did you hear of the death?'

'That's three questions,' smiled Pike, now back in command. 'I had occasion to phone Walter on Sunday. There was a slight problem with that article you've got a copy of, and his solicitor was in the house. He told me what had happened.

'As for the other part of your question, Walter years ago made me promise that I would contact the police in those terms if there were any question of sudden death.'

'You mean he didn't entirely trust the anonymity of the Raven?'

'I suppose he didn't in the last resort.'

'Did you like him?' asked Mason abruptly.

Pike paused. 'He said a lot of useful things,' he said at last.

'Acid has its uses?'

'Acid has its uses,' agreed Pike.

'Why did you call him "Professor" in your letter to my Chief Constable? He was a lecturer.'

'Did I? An inadvertent mistake on my part, I assure you.' But there was a glint in Pike's eye.

'Do you make mistakes?' Mason stared at him. 'Or might you have used to call him that to remind him of his failure?'

Pike laughed—almost a girlish giggle. 'So perceptive, my dear Superintendent.' He paused. 'You are quite right. I called him "Professor". That reminder, I felt, honed his edge.'

'Acid and razor images?'

'I would prefer to consolidate them—let us say he was a fine scalpel.'

'That's what Jack the Ripper used,' said Mason, getting to his feet. 'There is one other question,' he added.

'Yes?' Pike also rose to his feet.

'Did he choose the name for himself?'

'Yes. He used to make a joke about it—about being a raucous voice.'

'I can see that,' observed Mason thoughtfully. 'The raven is, however, quite a sociable bird among its own kind. Perhaps "crow" would have been a better choice. But then "raven" can be used as a verb. That would be not inappropriate.' Mason smiled, and left.

2

At lunch-time Mason met his son, Eric—all too briefly for the fond father. By six he was back home in Greyhavens, resisting the temptation either to swing round past headquarters, or to phone in to find out what had happened during his absence.

'That can wait,' Jane had said firmly as she drove out of the airport car park.

Next morning, however, Mason was up and at his desk early. He checked the computer for current developments. There had been some movement in the Emery case, but before checking the files he added an 'impression summary' briefly to the memos he had dictated while away. It wouldn't form part of the official papers, but he found it useful for himself occasionally to summarize his own impressions of interviews in a less formal fashion.

He went through the papers and memos on his desk. Alec Shepherd wanted to see him when he was available—fair enough. So did Harry Irwin. Mason paused at that. He never quite knew what to make of Irwin—he knew something of his background but was undecided about him. Sometimes he was angry with him, sometimes sorry for someone who had had a career go down the drain through drink and a failed marriage—whichever had come first. Still, Irwin was coming back from that, perhaps. But then there was also that connection with Lucrezia Gottman. What was Irwin wanting? He sighed. Perhaps he could spare a few minutes.

He pulled the Emery file to himself. Crawford had been busy. That was good. He was shaping up well.

After reading Crawford's report and the anonymous letter he sat back, drumming his fingers on his desk. So Gottman had been concealing information. It was more than an innocent forgetfulness—she was too intelligent for that excuse. And if that, how much more? Crawford was right. They would have to see her again.

He stretched. It was good to be back behind his own desk. He pulled his pad towards him and drafted a telex to the police authorities in Manchester, New Hampshire. Lucy Emery indeed. Black-haired. It would be interesting to know whether she was in the US—he reckoned that she must be about the same age as Lucrezia Gottman. What if Emery had, presumably unknowing, torn his own daughter's novel to pieces?

Just then there came a knock at the door and Alec Shepherd looked in.

'Convenient?' he asked.

'Sure. Come in. I'm just seeing what's been happening,' replied Mason indicating the papers spread before him.

'Paper breeds,' said Shepherd, dropping into a seat.

'You're early abroad?'

'It's never tomorrow until I've had my breakfast,' said Shepherd. 'I was out at the Amsterdam flight.'

'Incoming?'

'Yes.'

'And?'

Shepherd shook his head. 'We had a tip from over there, but there was nothing on that flight. We'll watch the five o'clock one as well.'

'What about the one that comes through Edinburgh?'

'That'll be dealt with there,' said Shepherd, stretching.

'How about coffee?' said Mason, checking his watch. 'The canteen'll be opening now.'

'Good idea.'

The two went down to the canteen. As they stepped out of the lift they heard the key being turned in the lock of the canteen door.

'I don't know how you manage to get your timing that accurate,' said Shepherd ruefully.

'Instinct,' replied Mason with a smile.

'You know, some of our younger colleagues think you've a crystal ball somewhere in your office,' Shepherd said as they settled down with their coffees.

'I wish I did. It would make things much easier.'

Shepherd nodded. 'But it'd be unlikely to be evidence in court.'

'Some of the things they now allow are like witchcraft. Take this DNA fingerprinting. That'll make life much easier.'

'I'm hoping it'll be some use in drugs. Though catching the users isn't rooting out the problem.'

'How's it going?'

'That's what I wanted to see you about.' Shepherd paused, marshalling his thoughts.

'Remember I said last week in court that we hadn't got the main supplier? We'd just got some of the foot-soldiers.'

'Yes.'

'And you're currently working on a death down at the Hydro at Monzie?'

'Yes.'

'Ever come across someone called Roy Grogan down there, though his real name is Mark Beddoes?'

'No. Not personally. What's the connection?'

'It may be nothing, but I was doing some cross-checking with the Home Office. This Mark Beddoes dropped out of sight a couple of years ago. He used to be a major runner working from North Africa, then he got into the organizing end of things. No one has seen hide or hair of him for a while.'

'And?'

'I don't suppose the name Colin Brown means anything to you either.'

'You're playing with me,' said Mason with a smile. 'I may not have a crystal ball, but I can feel when there's a trap being constructed for me.'

Shepherd grinned. 'He's in Greyhavens General.'

'The Saturday assault case?'

'Very good.' Shepherd shook his head disbelievingly. 'He was found on Saturday evening tucked away behind the electricity substation in Morison's car park.'

'Tucked?'

'Well, think of the place.'

Mason did and nodded. 'But why Morison's?' The name was that of a well-known firm of Greyhavens lawyers which had a car park close to their offices.

'No particular reason, except that it may be because it was close to Brown's flat.'

They sipped their coffee while Mason marshalled what he had been told. He put his cup down. 'So?'

'Brown seems to have been wanting to set himself up as a distributor—so the street rumour says. He was made an example of. A paving stone across the legs, including the right knee. He may need crutches for the rest of his life.'

Mason shook his head. Although he was used to such happenings, they never failed to shock.

'Has he said anything?'

'No. He wouldn't dare. I gather the common threat now is an injection with HIV blood.'

Silence descended on the two men. At length Mason spoke quietly.

'So you mentioned the name to him in hospital, and he reacted.'

'The name meant something to him, certainly. I'd bet quite a sum that Beddoes/Grogan is involved.'

'And he has something to do with the Monzie Hydro?'

'He's employed there, I gather. Your team interviewed him.'

Mason laughed. 'Ah well. Just goes to show you can't pick up everything. Come and we'll have a look.'

As they went up in the lift he asked, 'So what put you on to seeking him out?'

They went along the corridor to Mason's room. 'The name Mark Beddoes was given me from London. His *modus operandi* seemed to fit what we've been encountering. I'm nearly sure that he was in the public gallery for that drugs trial last week. It would fit—a sort of bravado.'

'How do you know that?'

'I don't know it, but there's a blurred street photo in the material I was sent from London. I always have a look at the public benches. It's a tip we were given. A trial's the criminal fraternity's chance to identify police officers if they're willing to take the risk. Conversely, it's our chance to identify them if they come.' Shepherd laughed. 'He was sitting beside Judgement Danny.'

Mason smiled. Judgement Danny was a local character who often appeared on the public benches in the local courts. He otherwise spent the time parading the streets with a bill-board carrying various Old Testament texts. 'They'd have a lot to say to each other. But tell me, how do you know your man is one of mine?'

'The Grogan alias was one of those among the London data—he's used five or six names, and has passports in all that we know of. You remember I had the use of Ian Crawford with that break-in at the Monzie chemist?'

'So you did.' Mason nodded.

'I saw him yesterday, and asked on the off-chance if you

had come across some of the names on my list. He checked for me, and there it was—Roy Grogan. QED.'

'That all?' asked Mason, opening the filing cabinet with the Emery files.

'Not quite. That Monzie burglary wasn't really serious, but it strikes me that they took the sort of thing that Beddoes might have wanted, if he's still in the business. Amphetamines mostly. There's still a market for them, and they're useful for leading idiots on to the more potent stuff. Some syringes went too.'

'That doesn't sound likely. If he is who you think—and that's not certain, though the name is unusual—he wouldn't foul his own nest, as it were—drawing attention to where it's not wanted.'

'Perhaps not.'

'Here we are,' said Mason, drawing out a sheet of paper from a bulky clipped set. 'I must get these in alphabetical order. Here you are. Roy Grogan, Entertainments Officer.' He passed it over to his colleague.

Shepherd swiftly scanned the page. 'Nothing of interest there,' he said, returning it. 'But I'd be obliged if you'd bear me in mind if anything turns up.'

'Don't scare him is what you really mean.' Mason's voice was dry. 'I'll bear it in mind.'

His phone buzzed. It was the front desk. Mr Irwin was downstairs asking to see him.

'Are we finished?' he asked Shepherd, who nodded assent and with a wave made for the door.

'What can I do for you that you can't get from the Press Office?'

Irwin was not abashed by his reception and sat without being asked. 'It's not information this time. I want you to do something for me,' he said, glancing around the room.

Mason was uncertain if this was inquisitiveness, or just that Irwin did not want to meet his eyes.

'Depends on what it is.'

'You're dealing with that death at Monzie.'

'Which death would that be? Statistically there have been a few in the last ten days or so.'

That worked. Irwin looked straight at Mason.

'I need help,' he said heavily. 'Your help.'

'Tell me,' said Mason in more sympathetic tones.

'You've met my niece Lucy—Lucrezia Gottman, that is. I know that. She told me. Seems to rate you quite highly though I can't think why.' He gave Mason a twisted smile. Clearly Irwin's spirit was recovering now that he had started speaking.

'Yes. I recall her. Long dark hair.'

'Just so. Well, I was in the bar at the Olympus last night when she came in. She was with a fellow who's a bad lot. He's in the drugs racket.'

'So?'

'So I'm worried what she's up to. She may be out of her depth.'

'Out of her depth?'

'She's got a hankering to break a big story—just like any cub reporter.'

'So? Are you telling me to watch out for her? Feed her a scoop?'

'I'd be grateful if you could warn her off.'

'Off what? I'm investigating a death.'

'Tell her to steer clear of her friend of last night.'

'I can't do that. If—say for the argument's sake, we assume that her companion is in the drugs business as you say—maybe she is too.'

'No. She's not the type.'

'Is there a type? We don't really see it, unless an overprivileged, overindulged youngster comes into that class.'

'No. She'd not be involved in that. I've heard her go on about what it did to friends of her down in London. She'd not be mixed up in anything like that.'

'So—again assuming this person is what you say—how can I interfere? I can't just say to her: "By the way, the person you were with last night is involved with drugs." If you saw her, why don't you speak to her?'

'I tried. I phoned her this morning, but all I got was a stone-wall. But you. You could say something. Warn her. It would carry weight coming from someone like you.'

'What did you say to her?'

'Just that her friend was up to no good.'

'Nothing about drugs?'

'No.' Irwin's head was down. 'I wasn't feeling all that well this morning.'

Mason knew what that meant. Irwin had a drink problem. 'And if what you say is wrong, what then?' he asked gently. 'I risk a defamation action.'

'She's got to be told,' came the sullen reply.

'She's old enough to pick her company. If you know some reason to challenge her choice, you'll have to deal with it.'

Irwin got to his feet, suddenly angry. 'I knew I shouldn't have come. But if anything happens to her I'll hold you responsible!' He banged the door behind him.

Shortly afterwards Shepherd knocked at the door.

'Here's the London data on Beddoes,' he said.

3

That afternoon Mason was sitting in the reserved room in the Monzie Hydro. He had briefed Crawford selectively on the way down about his trip and had been told in detail what had happened while he had been absent. Now he was waiting for Lucrezia Gottman.

The door opened. Crawford came in. 'She's not in the hotel,' he said.

'Does anyone know if she's gone out?'

'I know,' said Crawford. 'She'll be up the hill. She has a favourite spot.'

'Then get her,' said Mason with deliberate emphasis.

Crawford found her once more tucked into the nook overlooking the view.

'Superintendent Mason would like to have a word,' he said, rather stiffly. 'Down at the hotel.' He gestured to the path.

'After you,' she said. She got to her feet and followed. He felt very awkward but said nothing until at last when they were well into the hotel grounds he slowed up, forcing her to come up alongside.

'I'm sorry about this,' he said.

'So am I,' she replied with a bright smile and waving to someone on the tennis courts who seemed familiar to Crawford.

After Mason had reminded Lucrezia Gottman of what she had told him the previous Friday he sat back, steepling his fingers against his chin.

'Might it be that you would wish to alter, vary or correct anything of that?' he asked in a purring tone of voice.

She looked down at her hands which were clenched in her lap. Crawford opened his notebook. She drew a deep breath.

'I've been rather foolish,' she said, looking directly at Mason. Her open gaze seemed to rebound from his face, disconcerting her. She looked down again.

'What I said about coming here wasn't true. Your colleague here—' she gestured quickly to Crawford—'will have told you about that.'

Mason stayed still.

'I got a letter telling me that the Raven was Walter Emery, and that he was to be here. So I . . . I . . . I arranged to come.'

'Why did you not confront him at Wessex, or go to his home at Cancaster?'

'It was a matter of timing. When the letter arrived I just wanted to get hold of him as quickly as possible. He was coming here that weekend. I phoned. There was a cancellation.'

Mason dropped his hands to his desk. 'So there was a cancellation. How convenient. But you had known Emery before.'

'I was a student of his at Wessex.'

'Did you know anyone else when you came here?'

She was surprised. 'No. I'd never heard of the place.'

'Would you be surprised to know that you were one of several who got that letter?'

'I never thought of that.' She paused. 'I suppose I'm not likely to be the only one. Many people were injured by him.'

'Do you know who sent the letter?'

She shook her head.

'And you don't have the envelope?'

'No.'

He opened a file on his desk, drew out a letter and handed it to her.

'Read it again.'

She did so, then put it down on the table.

'Does anything strike you as odd about it?'

'No.'

'It's not actually your letter. It's one of the others. They all say the same, but in some the typing is of different widths.'

She pursed her lips.

'If I recall rightly you say that you were a reporter. What

I have said to you, and anything I may yet say, is and must remain strictly confidential.'

She nodded.

'You spoke to Emery on the main drive. Was that the first time?'

'No.' Again her voice was small, her head down.

'When before that?'

'The previous afternoon. I went up the hill and found him sitting on the seat up at the indicator at the top.'

'Were you out looking for him?'

She nodded. 'I had seen him in the dining-room the first evening, but I wanted to catch him somewhere private.'

'Did he recognize you up on the hill?'

'I don't think so—he was no good on faces.'

'What happened?'

She shrugged. 'I was so knotted up I couldn't say what wanted. I just said something fatuous like "Good day, Dr Emery" and went on. But I think even that rocked him. I looked back and he was staring after me. Trying to work out who I was, I suppose.'

'Then the next day you had your speech all worked out.'

'Yes.'

'Did you meet him accidentally?'

'No. I saw him go out of the front door, so I ducked down and went out by the lower door to the croquet lawn and from there walked up the drive to meet him.'

'And then?'

'And then I met him and said "Remember me? I'm Lucy Gottman." He brushed past me and went on down the hill. Then I ran after him and said my say. We were both quite heated.'

'What did he say?'

'He tried to tell me that criticism has to be an honest analysis of fault so that the writer can do better next time. I told him that in his case that was hokum. He just enjoyed eviscerating writers because he was impotent himself. I mean . . .' she broke off, blushing.

'You were speaking figuratively no doubt,' said Mason.

She nodded.

'Then you launched a broadside about his University career, my friend here tells me.'

Again she nodded.

'Anything else?'

'I don't think so.'

'Did you see or speak to him again after that?'

'No. At least I saw him and he must have seen me in the dining-room—but we didn't speak.'

'Or glare at each other?'

'I think we ignored each other, if anything.'

There was a pause. Mason shifted some papers on the desk as if searching for something.

'Why did you come back after leaving?' he asked.

'As I said before, it's a marvellous place and I'm writing a book.'

'Even though you knew Emery was here?'

'I asked a girl at the desk—as a favour before I left. She told me he was leaving on the Saturday.'

'Your novel is about murder.'

'Yes.' Her head rose as if to a challenge.

'And meeting Emery got you all fired up. It helped?'

She looked at Mason and then turned to eye Crawford, who kept his eyes on his notebook. 'That remains to be seen,' she said, 'but it's flowing quite well.'

Mason nodded pleasantly. 'I hope we'll see it in due course.' He paused. 'Would you like some coffee?'

'Yes, please.' She was surprised.

'Organize that, would you,' Mason ordered Crawford. 'See if you can get proper milk.' He turned to the girl as Crawford went out. 'I do dislike UHT milk, don't you?'

'It's awful.'

'Awful,' he agreed. 'Almost offal,' he went on, spelling out the last word.

She laughed.

'Your uncle's quite a fellow,' he said. 'Is he your mother's brother?'

'Yes. Daddy met her in London. Daddy's Hungarian—came West in 1956.'

Mason sighed—scratch one interesting theory. But if she was genuine, perhaps he owed her something. He got up and came round the table to stand beside her. 'Who were you with on Monday night?' His tone was suddenly urgent and serious.

She hesitated, then said, 'Roy Grogan. But how . . .'

'Never you mind. But could you not be more accurate?'

'How do you mean?'

'As to the name.'

She let out a deep breath. 'Mark Beddoes,' she said. 'He's calling himself Grogan for some reason.'

'Did you know he was here? Before you came?'

She put her hand on his sleeve and looked directly at him, forcing him to look at her. 'Has Uncle Harry been at you?'

'To coin a phrase, I ask the questions round here.' He tried to speak lightly.

'I knew it.' She moved impatiently.

'You may well be out of your depth.'

'With Mark?' She was at first incredulous, but then she thought and sighed. 'I wonder. It's been years.'

'And he can't have bought that car on what he earns here.'

She shrugged. 'He always was a wheeler-dealer.'

'Dealer may be right. Do you know something we should know?'

'Well . . .' She was hesitant. 'At Wessex . . .'

Mason sat down again. 'Perhaps we should wait till Ian gets back with the coffee.' Then he changed his mind.

'You were at Wessex with Mark Beddoes?'

She nodded.

'Both of you were taught by Dr Emery?'

Again a nod. 'Until Mark left. There was an awful fuss over an essay. Emery accused Mark of plagiarizing.'

'And when you came here and met Beddoes using a different name, that was the first you had seen of him since your student days?'

She shook her head. 'No. I used to see him occasionally at parties in London, until he disappeared.'

'Disappeared?'

'He just dropped out of sight.'

'What was he doing in London?'

'That was never clear. He used to say he was in "trade". He would say "trade" with that slightly deprecating laugh the upper class use.'

'So you don't know where he got his money?'

She sighed. 'No. There was some word of a rich and doting aunt, but . . .' She paused and then finished with a rush. 'But a fellow reporter—one of our investigative team —asked me once to tell her whatever I found out about him. The team thought he was mixed up in drugs.'

'Was he?'

'I don't know.'

'Is he?' Mason was intense.

She shook her head. 'I still don't know. There was something odd on Monday when I went to get my hairbrush from his car in Greyhavens. A couple of men were transferring a hold-all from his car to theirs when I arrived. But Mark— I mean Roy—appeared before anything was really said, and glossed over it. He said he was delivering tennis equipment. I didn't ask any more.'

'Would you recognize the men?'

'I doubt it. It was a fairly dim car park.'

'And I don't suppose you noticed the number of the car?'

She smiled. 'Training is all. It was a dark blue Ford.' She gave the number.

'Was he surprised when you turned up here?' Mason spoke while noting down the registration number.

'I'm not sure. He saw me before I saw him. Some time before.'

'How do you mean?'

'It was a kind of a mirror image of my meeting with Emery. I was up on the hill at the seat at the indicator watching the sunset. He ran up and sat down. "How are you?" he said—and it was Mark. Apparently he runs round the hill every evening.'

'You recognized him?'

'Oh, immediately.'

'Did you ask where he had been since his "disappearance"?'

'No. Of course not. I just said "long time, no see", and he laughed. He said he was now called Roy Grogan and asked me not to call him Mark. And that was that. He said he was working here—Entertainments Officer, or something like that. He organizes the tennis.'

The door opened and Crawford came back in with a tray. As he put the tray down on the desk Mason shook his head slowly from side to side to Lucy. 'Miss Gottman has been telling me about life in London. All those parties!'

'Sounds fun. All you ever hear about London is parties,' said Crawford as he straightened up.

'Actually it's mostly very boring,' she said.

'Mostly?' replied Mason. 'You'll need to be more specific. I've got a son who's gone down there for his first job. He keeps saying he works so hard there's no time for parties.'

'It's like that for an awful lot of people. I went to the parties, I think, mostly as a reporter.'

'Parties in line of duty. What an awful job.' Mason smiled.

'Now, how would you like your coffee? Did you say? I can't remember.'

But after supervising the coffee, Mason fell silent, going over what had been said, and leaving Crawford to carry the burden of conversation. Crawford found that difficult. He was confused. Mason did not seem to be nearly as annoyed with Lucy Gottman now as he had seemed earlier, even though she had in effect confessed to withholding information. Usually Mason was death on that. Maybe he was going soft?

When they were finished coffee Mason allowed Lucrezia Gottman to go, again warning her of the confidential nature of their conversation. 'That doesn't mean only that you're not to print it, or leak it to your confounded uncle,' he said, suddenly fierce—which again confused Crawford. 'An intelligent girl like you will also understand that you mustn't say anything about it to anyone.'

'I understand,' she said bleakly. 'I can put two and two together and get five too. It's just the hop between four and five that's difficult.'

'Good girl,' said Mason, patting her on the shoulder. 'I'll be back,' he threw over his shoulder, leaving Crawford behind. 'Get the files into the case.'

Upstairs he sought out Paton, the manager. 'It's about your Entertainments Officer,' he said. 'Can you tell me a bit more about the circumstances under which he came here? It was his aunt who recommended him? That's what you said in those staff notes.'

'Yes. It was quite fortuitous in a way. We were in a fix—the person we had engaged pulled out at the last minute and I was quite happy to take him on. He's been fine.'

'OK. Thanks. Not a word now, to anyone. Neither to him nor her,' Mason admonished.

'I just hope your questions don't lead where I think they do,' said Paton.

'Well?' asked Crawford as they drove back to Greyhavens.

'Well what?' responded Mason unhelpfully.

'What about "the truth always tells twice"?'

'What do you mean?'

'She's telling quite a different story now. And you said virtually nothing about that to her.'

'She's an intelligent girl. Before, she told us what she thought we needed to know. Now she's told us more because she sees things may be more serious than she thought.'

Crawford snorted.

'Wait!' said Mason, and stared out of the window.

Crawford snorted again, and maintained what he thought was a frosty silence all the way north. Mason did not notice. He was working with the jigsaw of knowledge. There were still some bits to turn over—were they sky, the most difficult, or what?

When he got back to Greyhavens Mason sent off two telexes and arranged to have the documentation on the Emery case looked at by Alec Shepherd and A. N. Drew. A separate note was sent to both.

Crawford was puzzled at the instructions and came in to check to whom the files had to go.

'Shepherd. Then Drew,' said Mason. Then he changed his mind. 'Keep the medical file out,' he said. 'Drew knows it, and I want to see whether Alec sees anything in the others that the forensic data is hiding from me.'

'Are you going to give me a clue?' asked Crawford.

'Wait and see,' was all that Mason would say.

'But what happens if you fall under a bus?' ventured Crawford.

Mason laughed. 'I think it's all there.' He waved a hand at the files on his desk.

'I don't know that I've seen all of it,' replied Crawford, somewhat put out.

'Bear with me. We'll confer with the others and decide what to do.'

'But . . .'

'But me no buts. Why me no whys,' replied Mason, astonishing Crawford by executing a stately pirouette before pushing him towards the door. 'Your Lucrezia understands,' he added.

'She's not my Lucrezia,' responded Crawford, but Mason thought he was not as vehement as he had been on the matter.

CHAPTER 11

FRIDAY

1

Two days later two unmarked police cars made their way through the upper gate into the grounds at the Monzie Hydro. 'Take the car up there,' said Mason, pointing to the right-hand road at the fork. Crawford did so, but looked inquiringly at his boss.

'We can leave the car up beside the stables. That way he shouldn't see it. Is that OK?' He turned to Alec Shepherd who was in the back seat.

'It's your show,' said Shepherd. 'Just get it under a tree.' He looked out at the blazing blue sky.

Crawford parked in the shade of a tree. Another anony-

mous car pulled up beside them. Mason went over to it.
'You stay here. Keep a channel open, and come if and when
we call,' he said.

'Right,' said the older of the two seated in it. 'Can we get
out and walk about a bit? Someone might think it odd if we
just sit in the car.'

'Good idea,' replied Mason. 'You could go over that way.'
He pointed to the fields beyond the stables. 'Have a look at
the horses. And you had better first check the lie of the land
round there.' He pointed to a stand of rhododendrons. 'Go
through that and across the road. The lower car park's
there. If he runs, it'll be towards his car. It's the yellow
sports car. Have a look, but don't go down till I say. Enjoy
the weather. Just don't come our way. Those radios are a
dead giveaway to those who know what they are.'

'Any word when we're getting a decently small radio?' he
asked Shepherd as he went back to the others.

'Not a clue. I saw a lovely little job one time I was down
south recently, but it's a matter of money.'

'Money,' snorted Mason.

Paton was waiting in his office.

'I've got bad news for you,' Mason said to the Manager
after he had introduced Alec Shepherd.

'I was afraid of that when you phoned,' replied Paton.
'There's been a feeling of something ominous hanging round
this place all morning. Somehow I wasn't surprised to hear
you were coming back.' He smiled without pleasure, waving
them to seats. 'You've been too thorough for that death to
have been quite as simple as it looked. And there were your
questions the other day. I take it that they have borne fruit?'

'I have a warrant in my pocket,' said Mason. 'We could
do things quite officially and by the book. But for various
reasons I would prefer something unofficial first.'

Paton was surprised. 'What do you want?'

'It's a search warrant,' said Mason. I need a look at his room. I think that will clinch things. But I want to look without him being present, if possible. If what's there is what we're looking for, then . . .' He gestured clutching at something. 'If not, then in fact it would be better for other reasons if there had been nothing official and if he didn't know. There are other inquiries going on which are connected with him, and we don't want to scare him off.'

Paton looked puzzled.

'I realize this must be very difficult for you,' Mason went on. 'He may be involved in drugs. If so, it's better he doesn't know we're taking an interest in him.'

'But . . .'

'I know: why don't we wait? The fact is that I may be going to charge your Mr Grogan with murder as well.'

Paton sat back, lifting his hands in horror.

Mason pressed on, using words to calm the man. 'It's like doing those sums at school. Remember teacher saying that ten includes nine and eight and all the other smaller numbers. Murder includes the smaller offences. Sometimes I think that drug-supplying is like a particularly bestial murder, but at present our lawgivers don't agree. But if we can convict Grogan of murder, that'll put him away for a substantial time. That alone would be good. I'm sure you see that.'

Paton nodded hesitantly.

'Did you know,' resumed Mason conversationally, 'that Al Capone was gaoled not for murder, extortion, prostitution or any of the other things he had done. He was sent away for evading taxes.'

He had Paton's interest. 'I didn't know that. I thought it was for the . . . the Massacre.'

'The St Valentine's Day Massacre? No, I'm not even sure that that was Capone. I think it was someone else.' He

turned to Crawford, who shrugged helplessly. 'Still, that's
not the point. Capone was gaoled for tax evasion, not for
any of the other crimes he clearly had perpetrated. Just so,
if Grogan is guilty of murder, we shouldn't wait to try to
get him for other things.'

'Quite so,' said Paton and sighed. 'Well, as it happens I
didn't have to make any arrangements to get him out of the
way. He's involved with the weekly tennis tournament. He'll
be on the courts until lunch-time at least.'

Mason checked his watch. 'That gives us a couple of
hours, to be safe.'

'I can arrange for you to be told if he comes early for any
reason.'

'I'd prefer not to have anyone else involved. Needs too
many explanations,' said Mason, dismissing the notion.

'I could do it myself,' said Paton.

'Well . . .'

'There's a room in the tower that we keep files and records
in. I sometimes go up there. It's got a view of the courts,
and it's only one stair below his room.'

'All right.'

Grogan's attic room was neat and anonymous, apart from
a half-empty modern bookcase and a surreal horror poster
on the end wall. A bed was against another wall. An old-
fashioned wardrobe and a chest of drawers stood behind
the door.

Mason looked about, a feeling of despair creeping over
him. Had he made a major mistake?

Crawford went over to the bookcase and looked along it.
'Here we are,' he said, picking out a paperback. It was
Frederick Forsyth's *Day of the Jackal*. 'You said he had a few
passports, sir.' He spoke to Shepherd. 'They say that this
book told quite a few people how to get birth certificates in
various names for use at the Passport Office.'

Shepherd took it and looked at it. Then he handed it back. 'That's not quite evidence,' he said drily, 'but I know what you mean.'

He turned to the bed. 'Here. Help me pull this out from the wall.'

Crawford did so, and Shepherd lay across it. 'Put on the light, Alan. I can't see a thing.'

Mason went to the window and looked out.

'What are you doing?' came Shepherd's voice.

'Just making sure we can't be seen from the tennis courts. I don't want him seeing a light up here.'

Shepherd grunted, and waited.

Once the light was on he worked his way along the floorboards. There was nothing of interest.

While Mason and Crawford put back the bed, Shepherd went over to the wardrobe and pulled it forward. Again he checked the floor and did the same with the bookcase. He shrugged, turning to the wardrobe.

Shepherd pulled out the heavily carved drawer that formed the base of the wardrobe. It came quite easily to about half way and then stuck. The drawer was full of jerseys, T-shirts and slacks. Shepherd knelt down and stirred the mess.

'Bingo,' he said.

'Eh?' responded Mason, coming forward.

'Feel the back,' said Shepherd, getting to his feet.

Mason did so.

'Now stand here,' said Shepherd, going over to one side.

Mason followed him.

'I'd say there's a cavity at the back of that drawer. Four inches, maybe a bit more,' said Shepherd, getting back down on his knees and running his hand along under the top of the drawer. 'Ah,' he said, and got to his feet again. He opened the top part of the wardrobe and scrabbled first at one side and then at the other under a pile of shirts and underwear. Then he stood back, concealing something in his hand.

'Try it now,' he said smugly.

Mason bent and pulled. The drawer slid forward, causing him to overbalance. Crawford helped him up.

'You see,' said Shepherd, holding out two pieces of wood shaped like 'T's about two inches long. 'That's what kept it from coming further out.'

Mason looked at the drawer. It had been fitted with a central partition, and as Shepherd had said, the back part was some four inches broad. In the cavity were two cakes of marijuana looking for all the world like rare old leather-bound books, a plastic packet of heroin, chemist's bottles of various sizes, two of them small and white, a couple of boxes, packets of plastic hypodermics, a green highlighter pen, two notebooks and a large book lying spine-down.

'I bet that's what you're looking for,' said Shepherd pointing at the small white bottles.

Mason took a plastic glove from his pocket, lifted the bottle, and nodded. He recognized the brand name as one Drew had given him. Sure enough the chemical data on the label listed phenelzine sulphate as the main ingredient. Mason smiled benignly. '"Protect from light", it says. He was certainly doing that.' He bent again and lifted and opened the large book. He showed its spine to Shepherd, then leafed through it a short way before stopping to read.

'Got it!' he said.

'What now?' asked Crawford after no explanation was forthcoming.

'We put it all back, and go and get him,' said Shepherd.

'No,' said Mason. 'Let's not disrupt the tennis. We can wait until its finished.'

*

The tennis overran. The three of them sat in the tower room among the records and junk of the Hydro and waited. Paton came up with a tray of sandwiches and coffee.

'It's unpleasant, this,' he said.

'Very,' replied Mason. 'I'm sorry to have inflicted it on you.'

'There's no doubt, is there . . . ?' Paton's hands fluttered.

'I'm afraid not,' said Mason uncommunicatively. He went over to Crawford who was on window duty. He looked over his shoulder then gave him a poke in the back.

'You're supposed to report anything of interest. That's La Lucrezia going up the hill?'

Crawford nodded. 'I wasn't watching for her.'

'Well, if you need anything else let me know,' said Paton, withdrawing. 'I'm sorry this place is rather dusty, but we only use it as a store now.'

'That's all right. It's ideal for our purposes,' said Shepherd, closing the door behind him.

'Do you suppose he burgled the chemist himself?' asked Crawford from the window.

'I doubt it,' said Shepherd. 'People like him get someone else to do the dirty work.'

'What about that book?' asked Crawford.

Mason smiled, wolfishly. 'It's the standard pharmaceutical reference text. Drew showed me his copy the other day. I checked the anti-depressant entries. Someone's used a green highlighter pen on the danger warnings for phenelzine sulphate.'

'There'll be prints on that pen,' began Crawford, but stopped as he saw Mason nodding.

'So it looks like it happened just as you thought,' said Shepherd.

An uncharitable observer might have categorized the expression on Mason's face as a smirk.

*

They had assembled in the conference room alcove.

'Right. You've all seen the files, or most of them. Let's start with the cause of death,' said Mason. He looked round at Alec Shepherd, A. N. Drew and Ian Crawford seated in the comfortable armchairs, then refreshed his memory from the pad on his knee.

'Either Emery died of a simple heart failure, in which case we've no reason to carry on the investigation. Or it was caused. Maybe it was triggered by the blow to the face. That may have been an accident—a matter of a fall in the room or elsewhere. The bruise is not conclusive on that?' He turned to Drew who shook his head.

'Alternatively, the blow happened during a quarrel with someone or other. We don't know who exactly. It could have been anyone—the receiver of another bad review hunting him out after one of those anonymous letters. Or someone that Emery annoyed quite separately and out of the blue—he had that capacity. But, in either case a charge of murder would be proper on the basis that you take your victim as you find him.'

He looked round the group again. The others waited.

'On site, as it were, we've got "X", someone completely uninvolved with Emery before the quarrel.' He held up his left thumb before dropping it. 'Otherwise, we've got as possibilities Lucrezia Gottman, who I can't see striking anyone unless in self-defence—' as he raised his right thumb he noticed Crawford nodding—'and Mark Beddoes/Roy Grogan.' He raised his right index finger. 'According to his interview with Paget, Grogan did not know who Emery was. That's not likely to be true. He'd have recognized Emery, though Emery may well not have recognized *him*. I think he was the person Emery quarrelled with on the Friday night.'

'Why don't we face him with that?' asked Crawford.

Mason sighed. 'You'd better study your Rules on Admissibility of Evidence again, laddie. We're at the stage of suspecting him of serious crime, and can't question without going through the full caution procedure. I'd prefer to see how much further we can get without that, first.'

Shepherd nodded sagely. Crawford flushed.

'Apparently Emery was responsible for Grogan's university career being cut off,' Mason went on. 'That would ground a row. Grogan would have seen Emery still apparently secure in his job and able to afford holidays at the Hydro, while he's got to work there. And if Grogan was the row on the Friday, he may well have struck Emery.'

'Is he a violent type?' asked Crawford.

'Yes,' said Mason. 'We know from the London file that he's not only got a temper, but a malevolent streak.'

'That didn't surprise me,' Drew intervened.

'I've a hunch that he ordered the attack on that ... what's his name?' Mason turned to Shepherd.

'Colin Brown. I think from what we know he's the linch-pin I've been looking for on that scene.'

Mason nodded. 'But to stick to the death at present. The chances are that it was Grogan's fist that caused the bruise, and maybe therefore the death.'

Drew leaned forward. 'A neat chain of perhapses,' he said. 'But there's the other matter.'

'Yes. Let's leave the assault aside,' resumed Mason. Finally, there's the drug that Drew found in Emery. What was it?' He made a pretence of turning for assistance to his notes.

'Phenelzine sulphate,' said Drew laconically.

Shepherd shifted in his seat and said, 'What's its proprietary name?'

Drew told him. Shepherd opened the file he was holding.

'Now we know that the deceased annoyed a lot of people by what were, on any fair reading, savage and often unfair reviews and articles. Being brutal seems to have been the man's life-blood,' continued Mason.

'I read a few of them,' said Drew. 'And I read some in the file. It's a wonder to me that someone didn't see if they could have him put under treatment. He was very close to paranoia.'

'Quite so. Academics seem peculiarly prey to that affliction. Emery was not promoted as he felt was his due. Then there is also the matter of the divorce. By the way, I've just had it confirmed by telex that neither the wife nor the daughter have been out of the US for the last three years, so that's them ruled out.'

'You are going for the murder option?' said Drew. 'Using the drug?'

'I'm afraid so. There's no proven method by which your drug could have got into him by medical treatment. Unless he was consulting a doctor we know nothing about, or got it from some herbalist or other.'

Drew leaned forward again. 'It *is* an anti-depressant. I suppose there is a chance he was depressed and—' he straightened—'maybe those articles were written under influence of the drug.'

Mason stared at him. 'You're not serious? That'd undercut everything.'

'No. I'm not serious. He doesn't sound as though he was depressed. From all accounts he vented his anger rather than letting it fester inside. But in any event I cannot see that anyone would have given him that drug in his condition. Not if they knew what they were doing. They would check his pressure automatically before putting him on that,' replied Drew. 'It'd be quite wrong for him.'

'Precisely. It's most unlikely that the drug was delivered innocently.'

'But in that case your list of suspects is enormous,' objected Shepherd. 'All those bruised authors. The wife and child—no, you've eliminated them. Other enemies? You've something in your notes about Wessex seeking to shed staff.

How would it be if a university were to cull its staff to meet its targets? There's a thought. Any university lecturer worth the name probably has the brains lying about to do a job like that. How are you getting where I think you're going?'

Mason leaned back. 'There's a principle of philosophy,' he said dreamily, 'known as Occam's Razor. Roughly speaking, the least number of elements required to explain a given circumstance—the most elegant explanation, as it were— is the correct one.'

'So what have you got up your sleeve?' asked Drew, getting a little impatient with his friend.

'You three, I hope,' said Mason with a smile. Crawford was flattered to be included. 'Help me. It must be Grogan. Confirm my hunch. Who'll start?'

'All right,' said Shepherd. 'Your crystal ball is working again. You asked me to bring the Monzie chemist burglary file and you asked Drew about phenelzine sulphate.' He flourished the file before opening it. 'A couple of bottles of that were taken at that break-in down there. A lot of other stuff went as well, but two bottles are in among that.'

Mason turned to Drew. 'So that would be the source,' he said. Drew nodded, and smiled. He extracted from his pocket a white pill bottle, uncapped it and spilled on to the table some ovoid, orange pills, which looked for all the world like children's sweets.

'That's them,' he said.

Mason turned back to Shepherd. 'It would perhaps help if we could find out whether the burglars cleared out all that they had of the tablets, or if just the couple of bottles were taken.'

'I imagine that it might be the whole supply,' said Drew. 'There's not much call for it in fact and it'd be the sort of thing that you could get quickly from a wholesaler.'

Mason grunted. 'Now we've got phenelzine whatsit going

missing down in Monzie and some turning up in Emery a few days later. How might that happen? I don't suppose they're like sweets, though they look like it.'

Drew leaned forward. 'That's not entirely impossible. Suppose that he were offered . . . but no. They're not like sweets.' He sat back slowly. 'The most efficient way, if you can't get them into him in the normal way, would be to—' He banged his hand on the table. 'And I allowed the bathwater to be drained.'

'Bathwater?' Mason was incredulous.

'No. No. Not what you think. But if the phenelzine were in that tea that Emery had with him, that could do it, if the concentration were high enough.'

'Which takes us to the UHT milk. Would it dissolve in that?'

'Not very well. Enough to cause an upset, but not more.'

'Which is what we had in those other cases.'

Drew nodded. 'It would taste funny. But then UHT milk does taste funny.'

'Wait a minute,' said Mason, and opened another file. 'I have it.' He grinned at Crawford. 'The value of lists,' he said to him while passing the file over to Drew. 'Look at that.' He pointed at a sheet in the file.

'In that case,' said Drew, having read the list, 'I think I can complete your picture. You're right in a way. You have got us up your sleeve.'

They were coming to the end of the sandwiches when Crawford spoke again.

'That's it. They're done.'

Mason drew his radio from his pocket. 'Right. We're in business. Go down to the lower car park.'

'Understood,' came the reply.

The three walked between the tennis courts, threading their way through spectators and competitors who were heading for lunch. Grogan was at the upper gate to the west set of courts speaking to a couple.

As they turned the corner he caught sight of them. He stopped speaking, stared, then turned and ran. Up the hill.

'Damn,' said Shepherd. 'He must've recognized me. Where does that go?'

'He could cut across to the main road,' began Mason, but Crawford interrupted.

'Lucy's up there,' he threw over his shoulder as he started to run.

A remote portion of Mason's mind noted the use of the familiar name. Mason was not fit, but he soon left Shepherd behind. He followed the sound of the two, crashing their way up the hill.

Out of the trees and up on the flat top of the Knoll he saw Crawford gaining on the other. Through the pounding of his temples, he heard Crawford's shout. 'Lucy! Look out!'

The girl rose into sight. She had been sitting at her favourite spot. The two men were closing on her. Mason saw Crawford make a final diving lunge, tripping Grogan, but the momentum of the other carried him forward. The girl threw herself to one side, and Grogan disappeared.

Mason slowed down, walking the last fifty yards or so. Crawford helped the girl to her feet, then enfolded her in his arms, turning her away from the scene. She buried her face in his shoulder.

Mason went to the edge, and looked down.

2

Later that afternoon Mason went to see Mrs Murgatroyd. She was sitting beside her window, suddenly a little old lady.

He spoke without preamble. 'I am sorry to have to tell you that your nephew is under arrest.'

She bowed her head. 'For . . .' she asked.

'He has not yet formally been charged but it is in connection with the death of Walter Emery and with various
offences related to drugs. I am also sorry to have to tell you
that he has been seriously injured attempting to evade
arrest.'

She sighed. 'I feared as much. I saw all the commotion
earlier.'

'You saw?'

'I saw you and two others going up to the tennis courts.
I saw Mark run. Susan told me there had been an accident
on the hill. She saw the ambulance. How is he?'

'Not very good, I'm afraid,' replied Mason, coming over
to stand beside the old woman. 'It will take time.'

Then he gave way to the question that had been worrying
him for four days.

'You suspected? You knew?'

She sighed again. 'He was an engaging child, with such
a naughty streak in him. It appealed to me.'

'What did you know of his activities lately?'

'Nothing, really, but I had fears. A friend in London
wrote to advise me. She had seen him at some parties and
suggested that he was getting into deep waters, so I arranged
to have him come here to the job. Mr Paton was most
obliging. Is suited us both. I wanted him somewhere close
and away from London. They needed someone to arrange
the tennis and such things. Someone had cried off at very
short notice. Mr Paton told you?'

'Only after I asked,' Mason prevaricated.

She nodded, satisfied by the reply.

'And Emery?' prodded Mason.

'Ah yes. That was unfortunate. I mean un-fortunate.
Unlucky. I had forgotten that Mark had been at Wessex.
Walter was responsible for getting him sent down. At least
that's what Mark told me. He was very angry.'

'But why didn't you tell me this before?'

'Blood is thicker than water, I suppose. I did try. But when I saw you, and your sternness underneath that charming manner, I just couldn't. I told you there was someone upsetting Walter. After that it was up to you. Did I do wrong?'

Mason swiftly reviewed mentally what had happened. Could it have happened better? Perhaps that boy back in Greyhavens might be walking still. Perhaps young Master Farrell down in Bristol would still be waiting for his birth day. Perhaps not.

Mrs Murgatroyd seemed to follow his thought. She levered herself to her feet and crossed to the fireplace where she pressed the bell.

'Will you take tea with me?' she asked.

3

'So who tied it up for you?' asked Jane later that evening. Mason had come in grim-faced and without the usual bounce that marked his step when a case had been dealt with, and they were sitting together at the table in the kitchen nook after dinner.

'That was the conference,' replied Mason, stirring himself. 'Yesterday. We had various things to check before we could act, lest we scared him off.' He outlined the deliberations.

'But I don't understand,' said Jane. 'What did Drew-Drew mean by saying you had them up your sleeve?'

'He remembered that Roy Grogan, or Mark Beddoes as we should call him, doubled as a conjuror for the Friday night entertainment. "The hand is quicker than the eye", you know. During the argument, he removed the teabags in Emery's room and replaced them with a single bag which he had opened earlier and laced with powdered phenelzine tablets. He'd crushed the tablets with a couple of spoons.'

'How do you know it was the teabag?'

'Well, we've established minute traces of the drug in the used tea-bag. Not much, for it'd been in the water for hours. However, Grogan's confirmed it. But apart from that Drew spotted the tea as the vehicle, and I remembered something. There were no teabags on Crawford's inventory of the room, and none among Emery's effects. Only the used one in the bath. While Crawford and I were in Emery's room that morning a maid said something about people taking away the tea and coffee, but it didn't click until the meeting. There was only one teabag in the room. That shows giving the drug was intentional. Clearly Emery was intended to ingest it that night—he was leaving the next day. And he was known to love tea.'

'It also shows the quarrel may have been spurious—if Grogan went prepared.'

'True.'

'Might it have been done as a joke?'

'No. There's no way it was just a joke.'

'Still, it might have been intended to frighten, not to kill. Just to give him a jolt. Would Grogan have known Emery's medical condition?'

'I don't know. But in law if you assault someone and he dies because of some inherent condition, you are properly charged with murder. Still, I suppose it'll be up to Crown Office to decide how to proceed. It'll be difficult for them. Very difficult.' He became pensive again.

'Is this drug tasteless?' asked Jane, trying to stir him.

'No. But Emery suffered from catarrh and, thanks to a bungled nasal operation years ago, he'd little sense of smell. Smell is a major portion of taste, so I'm told he wouldn't have noticed the odd taste.'

'And the other cases?'

'That's the "offal" joke. That was too literary, pointing

to someone with an educated background. Grogan laced
some of the UHT cartons with a weak solution of the
phenelzine, using a syringe—probably one of those stolen
from the chemist. I expect he was surprised to find the
police taking an interest in the death, and hoped we would
think it was an accident because of some nut campaigning
against UHT milk. He probably smuggled it into the pantry
for those rooms.'

'And Mrs Murgatroyd?'

'I'm not sure. We haven't got round to that. At its worst
he might have hoped she would die—after all, she knew the
connection with Wessex, and he may have heard that I was
talking to her. On the other hand it might be that he just
spread the UHT cartons about and she was unlucky. We've
had them all withdrawn, and they're being checked.'

'But how do you know it was this man? What about the
woman, the one with the odd name?'

'She didn't react to the "offal" joke when I made it to
her. And there's nothing else to tie her in. Her parentage is
as she said it is—Somerset House confirmed that within
twenty-four hours. She was foolish in coming up here to
confront Emery, and then arguably more so in coming back
to investigate Grogan/Beddoes, though she couldn't have
known what she was getting into. She was out of her depth,
as Irwin thought.'

'Irwin?'

Mason explained the connection. 'But you'll be able to
see for yourself. She's going to move up here to stay with
him for a few weeks. I think we'll maybe invite her and Ian
Crawford round for dinner.' He smiled, but Jane paid no
attention.

'So you can *prove* it was Grogan who switched the teabag,
if he retracts?'

'I can't really pin it down one hundred per cent, but it is
beyond reasonable doubt, I think. It was male voices argu-

ing in Emery's room that night. The drug was concealed in Grogan's room. His prints are on the bottle and on the highlighter pen. That chemist's book is marked.'

'Careless. Or over-confident.'

'He was somewhat. To have taken someone you knew was a reporter on a delivery run into Greyhavens . . .'

Mason whistled.

'Camouflage?'

'I suppose so. But that's an end of that.' He was silent again.

'And Grogan's confirmed it?'

Mason nodded.

'That seems out of character.'

'I didn't tell you the worst. He was anxious to talk once we got to him.'

Jane looked at her husband. He was very solemn.

'When he ran, he ran up the hill. It was Crawford who realized that he was going for Lucrezia Gottman. She was usually up the hill at a favourite spot beside that cliff—you know, looking out over the valley.'

Jane nodded.

'He recognized Alec Shepherd and thought we were there about the drugs. He knew she had seen something in the car park, and I suppose he thought she had reported it. He'd seen her with Ian too.' His voice went thoughtful. 'He wanted to punish her.'

He paused. Jane waited.

'Crawford managed to trip Grogan as he got to her. She threw herself to one side. Grogan missed her. You know the place.'

Jane shuddered.

Mason's tone was bleak. 'He's broken his back. Quadriplegia. He'll never do anything for himself again.'

'Will they put him on trial?'

'I expect so. It'd be in the public interest to try both the drugs and the murder charges. I'm glad I don't have to decide about that. That's a matter for Crown Office.' He paused. 'It's odd, you know.'

Jane looked at him. He continued in a dreamy voice: 'It's odd. When we got down to him, there was a raven sitting on a rock near him. It wouldn't go away. We tried to drive it off while we were waiting, but it just fluttered about as he talked—on and on. I'd swear it ducked a stone I heaved at it. Then just as Grogan was lifted on to the stretcher it started croaking—Crawford swears it was laughing.'